# NO FARM NO FOWL

JULIE ANNE LINDSEY

Cozy Queen
PUBLISHING

# A NOTE FROM THE AUTHOR

Hello Lovely Reader,

Thank you so much for joining me on Thelma & Louisa's first adventure! It's been a ton of fun seeing side characters from my Bonnie & Clyde Mysteries spinoff and get involved in investigations of their own.

Don't forget to keep in touch between the books via my Cozy Club newsletter.

And if you enjoy NO FARM NO FOWL and want to see where Thelma & Louisa got their sleuthing starts, pick up book 1 in the Bonnie & Clyde Mysteries, BURDEN OF POOF.

Now, it's time to meet your new favorite feathery little sidekick!
    -Julie Anne Lindsey

## CHAPTER ONE

"*J*ill!" I called, smiling brightly as I approached my favorite brunette.

She'd been a little down since her family left town, and I had a fantastic idea I hoped would cheer her up.

Jill turned in my direction, watching me suspiciously, as I made my way to her side. In fairness, she was right to give me that look. I was up to something.

"So, I was thinking," I said, stopping at her side. "You and Jack should get married."

She snorted, and I raised a palm. "Hear me out. I wouldn't normally suggest a woman marry the only man she knows, especially as a way to improve her mood, but a miniature donkey wedding will be the most adorable thing that has ever happened in our community," I cooed, slipping into baby talk as I pleaded. "And I know Jack will agree."

I grabbed her brush from the bucket where I kept her grooming supplies before she could nip or kick me and began to smooth her coat.

Jack munched hay nearby, eyeballing us warily as we spoke.

I'd inherited the set of miniature donkeys when my neighbors moved away. It'd been sad to see the family leave their animals behind, but not everyone had room for livestock, I supposed.

"But seriously, Jill, Jack is an amazing companion, and he clearly adores you. Plus, let's face it, I've been dreaming of a wedding like this all my life. I can be ordained online in about thirty minutes, internet signal strength permitting. All of Meadowbrook will come. You'll get gifts. I've already asked Thelma to be your maid of honor."

*Bawk-ah!* Thelma, my sassy Polish hen and the best feathered friend a lady could have, pecked and scratched at the ground near my feet. She was never one to roam far or miss an opportunity for girl talk.

"See?" I asked Jill. "Thelma's excited, and everyone knows Jack only wants what you want. So, what do you say?"

"Louisa!" My neighbor Mary called to me from outside the donkeys' tiny stable.

I glanced through the small window, then set the brush aside. "Think about it," I said, offering Jill a parting pat.

She nuzzled her head against my side as I turned to leave.

"Careful or I'm going to take that as a yes," I told her.

"Louisa," Mary called again, stopping short of the open barn doors. "Great. There you are."

I raised a hand to shield my eyes as I moved outside to meet her. My skin instantly warmed, thanks to an industrious southern sun.

Meadowbrook, my small cottagecore community, lay out like the pages of a storybook around us. The hundred or so residents lived in communal harmony, with themselves, with others and with nature. We were a neighborhood of sorts, within the larger outdoorsy village of Cromwell, Georgia. But folks who lived in Meadowbrook chose to live off the land and through the combined efforts of self and others as much as possible. According to pop culture the cottagecore lifestyle was a modern romanticizing of rural living. To us it was simply the peaceful way of living.

"Have you seen this?" Mary asked, waving her cell phone as she finished the trip to my side.

Some Meadowbrook citizens were naturally more peaceful than others.

Mary's long crimson dress swished hard against her lace-up boots. Her pretty features were set in a seething grimace.

I stood a little taller, preparing to deflect her mood with sheer willpower and positivity.

Dark hair flew around her face like storm clouds in the wind. Her jade-green eyes flashed with their usual, though somewhat heightened, irritation.

"Good morning," I returned, offering a small wave. I folded my hands against the crisp fabric of my vintage lemon-print sundress. "I suppose it's afternoon," I said. My souffle stand had been closed nearly an hour, and I'd locked up around eleven.

"Speaking of your budding enterprise," she said. "That enormous knucklehead, Frank Flint, called Souffle the Day awful and common with no frills." She stopped before me and crossed her arms, a basket of eggs hanging from the crook near one elbow. "Awful with two Ls, because apparently he can't spell and he's got terrible opinions."

I forced a tight smile and sought the silver lining. "I suppose it's a little true. I was never going for frills," I said, thinking of the simple but inviting décor. "I didn't realize he planned to post a critique. He seemed happy while he was here. He even called my shop a new option for delicious, affordable breakfasts."

I'd hoped the article would increase business, as well as improve relations between Cromwell citizens and those of my community. But that had clearly been too much to ask.

Souffle the Day had been open almost three months, and I was still learning the ropes as a restaurateur. Before then, I'd simply bred my Polish hens for income and traded their eggs within Meadowbrook for things I needed. Problem was, not everything I needed could be swapped for eggs. Wi-Fi for example. Selling quiches and souffles for cash, on the other hand, paid the bills.

"How are you so calm about this?" Mary asked.

"I'm processing, I guess."

Mr. Flint had spent several mornings with me, observing business at the souffle stand and observing life in motion at Meadowbrook. He'd even made notes about the way my new café encouraged Cromwell residents, or townies as we called them, and members of my community to interact. He'd predicted the time folks spent mingling would go a long way toward breaking down unfair judgments on both sides.

Mary huffed and the basket swung once more.

I smiled. Mary and I were both twenty-six, and we loved our community, but we were opposites in every other way. I'd grown up in Cromwell, but Mary came from somewhere up north, based on her accent. She didn't talk about it. Her hair was black, mine was blond. Her catlike eyes were green and challenging. My wide, round eyes were blue and full of faux innocence. I envied her warm olive skin and perpetually dewy complexion. My skin was painfully fair and perpetually sunburnt. Not to mention the way I blushed at the slightest provocation or exertion.

And Mary was a little mean.

Profound differences aside, we'd bonded after she attempted to save my life not long ago and I'd helped her while she healed from the resulting injuries. Our love of hens had helped. Mary raised Plymouth Rock chickens with black-and-white barred feathers that made them look like a bunch of birds in old-timey prisoner costumes. My Polish hens had the glorious bouffants of ladies who'd just left a Dolly Parton- and Elton John-run salon.

"You can't just smile politely through this one," Mary warned. "This is serious. You've barely been open three months, and this guy's garbage article is going to turn people away. I knew Cromwell should never have gotten a website."

The town council had recently voted to launch a site for tourism and communication purposes. Folks were split on the idea. Most thought the overwhelming beauty of our mountains, river and national park were enough to draw outdoorsy tourists without the additional expense and upkeep of a website. Others, specifically every small business in town, jumped on the opportunity to reach a wider audience with all they offered.

I'd been thrilled to learn an associated food blog would feature local cafes and restaurants. I was beginning to rethink my enthusiasm, not that I'd admit that to Mary.

"Everyone reading this terribly written article about how unpleasant it is to eat eggs in a pasture will immediately decide never to come here. Then you'll be back to trading eggs for goods, and I'll be out of a paycheck. Again!"

"It's too soon to panic," I said. "And there are other places who will buy your eggs if this article single-handedly sinks my shop, which it won't."

Mary made a dark, throaty sound. "Do you like having Wi-Fi? Because last I checked, you can't trade soap for that."

My smile drooped a bit, because she was right on that point, and I loved having good Wi-Fi.

I rolled my shoulders and refreshed my smile. "I'm sure no one even visits the town website. And those who do aren't relying on a food column called Local Yum for advice on where to eat."

Mary raised a perfectly manicured brow. "And what about the *Cromwell Chronicle*?" she challenged, stuffing a hand into her apron pocket and pulling out a neatly folded square of newspaper.

I accepted the offering with trepidation, then unfolded it for a better look at the problem. The headline in today's Local section was:

Do Eggers's Souffles Fall Flat? Cromwell Critic Cracks Back

An image of my café anchored the letters. "This doesn't seem so bad."

"Except that Flint said your whole experience falls flat." Mary waved one hand in a broad circle, apparently indicating everything in sight.

I turned my eyes back to the article, skimming the words and cringing at direct quotes pulled from Local Yum. "Cows eat in pastures, people should not," I read. "Save yourself the trip and the money. Eat in town."

"Now can we, please, go find and throttle this guy?" Mary asked, setting a hand on her hip when I looked up.

I rubbed my forehead, smoothing the deep crease that had formed. "It wasn't his best writing."

"It's awful," Mary agreed. "Why isn't anyone critiquing that? Regardless, you can't let him get away with an attack like this."

I refolded the paper, attempting to order my thoughts. "It doesn't sound like an attack. It's more like a report of personal opinion." Which is exactly what a review was meant to be. I'd gotten the impression he liked what I'd done here, but clearly I'd misread him. "Maybe some folks will read this and like the idea of eating in a pasture."

"Like cows?" Mary asked.

"Like people who enjoy nature and appreciate the beauty around them. Cows included. So, no. We're not throttling Mr. Flint until there's good reason to do it." Even then, a verbal lashing was as violent as I got, and that wouldn't come until I'd had a chance to ask politely about his review.

A heavy breeze ruffled the fields of wildflowers and freshly tended flower beds, sending scents of azaleas and hyacinths to my nose. It was impossible to get too upset when nothing bad had actually happened. My gaze caught the silhouettes of our neighbors working merrily in their yards, tending to their animals and enjoying the peacefulness of our little earthly nook.

I recentered myself and returned the paper to Mary. "Looks like rain is coming."

She checked the deep blue sky and fat gray clouds overhead.

Reluctantly, I added, "I'll call Wilhelmina at the *Chronicle* and ask her for a proper write-up, to counter any negativity Flint's review and her recap caused. She seems like a nice, reasonable woman. I'm sure she'll understand one man's opinion shouldn't be the final word for my new business."

Wilhelmina was older than my grandmother and Cromwell's only events and crimes reporter. The village had little of both, so it was a part-time gig at best and likely left her hard up for content. "Maybe I can get her out here for Jack and Jill's wedding," I said, renewing a hopeful expression. "I can cater using Souffle the Day menu items. Everyone will see Meadowbrook is a charming community, and my souffles are delicious."

Mary curled her lip and shoved the basket of eggs in my direction. "Here. These are for the café, assuming anyone comes back."

"Thanks."

"I'm going home to get my yardwork done before the rain," she grouched, then waved a hand as she turned away. "Figure this out."

My shoulders drooped as she crossed the lawn toward

her home. Mary was outwardly sullen and often unapologetic, but she was sincere and loyal to a fault. I suspected her life before Meadowbrook hadn't been pleasant. And I wanted her to feel safe and secure here, financially and otherwise. "I'll fix this," I called belatedly. "Everything will be okay."

The sky darkened dramatically as I spoke the words, and I pushed aside the idea it was an omen.

Mary glanced back over her shoulder, eyes darting to the horizon as she spoke. "You left the lights on at the stand. You should probably turn those off and save the money. Won't be able to afford that kind of excess much longer."

"Everything will be fine," I repeated. "Don't worry."

Mary rounded the side of my house, vanishing from view, and I worried a little for Mr. Flint's safety if I was wrong.

I turned toward my souffle stand with a sigh. A light was still visible inside. I hadn't meant to leave it on, and I hadn't noticed its glow before the storm clouds moved in. I supposed I was thankful for the untimely darkness because Mary was right, electricity wasn't cheap. And I couldn't trade eggs or goat soap for that either.

"Well, Thelma," I called to my sweet brown-and-white hen now mingling with her sisters near the pen. "I don't suppose you want to round up the flock while I turn off that light. Rain's coming."

*Bawk-aw!* She ruffled her feathers and cocked her head my way, then began a series of steady clucking.

"Fine. I'll do both," I said. "Be back in a minute." I pulled the length of my dress away from my feet as I dashed across the field. There were so many freedoms for me in Meadowbrook. So many things others took for granted. Like the freedom to play in the rain. To wear dresses smudged by the evidence of an afternoon spent with hens and little donkeys. To be part of a community that understood why such simple things were so precious.

The first rumble of thunder arrived as I unfastened the lock on my souffle stand, freeing the double barn doors. The oversized outbuilding was roughly large enough for two or three farm trucks parked side by side, a three-car garage with arched rafters. The structure had initially sheltered a small tractor, various tools and supplies. I'd cleaned the place out and reinvented it as my roadside shop, complete with small utilitarian kitchen, nostalgic egg-and-flower-themed décor and a few tables. Most folks opted to sit at the picnic tables I'd arranged outside, where air could better circulate.

The doors groaned open, and I stepped in, knocking the switch to OFF.

The room darkened, and an unexpected shiver wiggled down my spine. Possibly a result of electricity in the air caused by the brewing storm.

A clap of thunder and simultaneous slam of the utility door across the way caused me to jump. The door bounced gently in the growing wind, while I struggled to catch my breath.

I never used the utility door, but today someone had.

## CHAPTER TWO

*A*s Mary predicted, business was slow the next morning. I didn't even need the frozen souffle batter I'd stocked the day before.

It wasn't clear if the lack of customers was a result of the unflattering article in yesterday's paper, the online review posted the day before that, or happenchance.

I wasn't a big believer in happenchance. And both of the other two options were bad.

I dragged my gaze over the small shop. A peppy blue, white and yellow theme ran throughout the space, from checkered tablecloths to draperies and everything in between. All colors designed to make people happy. To improve their days and prepare them for an amazing breakfast experience.

Even if it was in a pasture.

Framed photos of my friends, neighbors and hens hung on the walls beside displays of antique pans, kitchen gadgets and baskets handwoven in Meadowbrook.

I alternated wiping counters and checking the clock while fussing internally over the cause of my slowest day on record. And trying not to wonder if my mother saw the bad review.

When I couldn't stand the uncertainty anymore, I dialed the *Cromwell Chronicle* and asked for Wilhelmina.

"Hmm," the man on the other end of the line hummed over my question. "It looks like she won't be in until closer to lunchtime. She left a note on her desk about popping in and out and chasing a story."

I rubbed my forehead, unsure if I hoped I was the story or not.

Definitely, if she was planning a follow-up piece with kinder words.

Definitely not, if she planned to confirm Mr. Flint's critical comments.

"Thank you," I said. "I'll drop by around lunchtime and see if I can catch her."

"Sure thing. I'll let her know. Who's calling?" I bit my lip, afraid she might prefer to dodge me after yesterday's write-up. Wilhelmina didn't know me. She only knew my mother. "Oops," I said, unable to give my name. "There's someone at my door. I'm going to have to call you back."

I disconnected and closed my eyes for a long beat. In the future, I needed to keep a list of pre-planned verbal escapes at the ready for situations like these.

Fortunately I'd have plenty of time to brainstorm ideas while my business continued filling with crickets.

I looked around the silent outbuilding, heart breaking for a multitude of reasons. I'd dreamed of opening this café for ages, and I'd planned every detail from general operations to product production, but I hadn't prepared for a single unflattering article to derail all my work.

The success or failure of Souffle the Day reflected on more than just me. My entire community had supported and encouraged me. They shared my wins and losses. Even a second-chance shop owner in the neighboring village had a stake in this. She'd helped me turn an ugly old outbuilding into a place worthy of ordering breakfast. And whether I wanted to admit it or not, a portion of my family's money, courtesy of a trust I typically pretended not to have, had helped as well.

I didn't want to let anyone down, myself included. So this was a fight I'd have to suit-up for.

I flipped the OPEN sign to CLOSED a few minutes early and prepared to get my customers back. I wasn't sure what that would take, but I was a fully grown, educated, head-strong woman. And I hadn't come this far to fail.

I double-checked the utility door and made certain all the light switches were set to OFF before stepping outside. It'd taken a few minutes the night before, but I'd eventually realized the rear door had probably been unlocked since the days when renovations were still underway. Wind from the storm had jostled it open. Nothing had been taken or damaged. I'd just overreacted.

"Thelma," I called, crossing the thick green grass back to my cottage. "Want to go to town?" Most pet lovers toted cats or dogs with them, but I loved Thelma. And she loved to travel, so we went most everywhere together.

*Bawk-ah!*

I grabbed my bicycle from where it stood beside the patio. Meadowbrook had a communal pickup we shared to reduce our group footprint, but I had energy to burn.

I tucked Thelma into her crate, then secured it in the large basket fixed to the front of my bike. And we were on our way.

Air pocketed beneath my skirt as I pedaled along the paved roads toward town, billowing the soft white fabric and cooling my legs as they pumped. I soared over hills and around curves until the familiar lineup of box-shaped shops came into view.

Thelma clucked steadily as we rode, singing her own traveling song or praying for her life, I wasn't sure which. I could only imagine the view from her crate as I navigated the downtown traffic, passing stinky log trucks larger than the hen house she shared with a dozen cousins and sisters.

I stopped at a bike rack near the Main Street bridge and admired the view. Cromwell was built at the edge of a lake, along the finger of a river and beside a national forest. It was a place steeped in history and tradition but also obsessed with the outdoors. Stinky log trucks aside, the town was perfection.

I locked my bike in the rack, then unloaded Thelma's carrier and marched toward the newspaper office with my chin held high. "Here goes nothing," I told her, then silently ran through what I would say to the reporter.

*Good morning, Ms. Wilhelmina. We haven't spoken in years, and you probably don't remember me, but I'm Louisa Eggers. Yes, that's right. Victoria Eggers's daughter. Yes. She scares me too. No, she doesn't know I'm here. No, there's no reason to panic. I'm nothing like my mama.*

Mama was the embodiment of all wealthy-southern-women stereotypes. She embraced them. Aspired to be more perfectly aligned with them. Led those who aimed to be like her and destroyed all in opposition. In short, she was a pillar and a legend, as most quality villains were.

I'd moved to Meadowbrook following college graduation. Dad had stopped coming home shortly afterward, the frequency and duration of his business trips had grown as I did, until one day, we were both gone for good. Some days I was glad I'd been the one to leave first, because I wasn't sure I could've left her alone if Dad had beaten me out the door. Other days, I wished I could do the right thing and go back, because I knew she needed someone to look out for her. Mostly, I tried not to think about it. I was enjoying life on my terms. And when the day came and Mama passed, I'd take my rightful place at Laurelwood, the estate my ancestors had built.

Assuming Mama's sheer power of will hadn't made her immortal.

The door to the newspaper offices swung open, and I yanked my hand back, having reached for the knob. Thelma's crate wobbled with the jolt.

*Bawk-ah!*

"Oh!" A short, narrow man in a pink polo shirt and khakis raised both hands in shock. "Whoopsie," he said, chuckling nervously. "I was just on my way to lunch. Can I help you?"

"I hope so," I said, eyeballing the little white cottage that served as home to the *Cromwell Chronicle*. "I'm hoping to catch one of your reporters."

The man scrutinized me and my bedazzled pink pet carrier.

"Is there a chicken in there?" he asked.

*Bawk-ah!*

"That's Thelma," I said. "Is Wilhelmina here? I called earlier."

He dragged his eyes back to mine. "No. I'm sorry. Wilhelmina hasn't come in as planned. I'm not sure when she'll be around, to be honest."

I groaned, hot and thirsty from a bike ride in the sun. "Did she say when she might be in? I'm happy to come back in an hour or so if she's just running late." Thelma and I could stop at a local café for drinks, then visit a park where she could stretch her legs. We could circle back to the newspaper again afterward.

The man shook his head. "I don't even know if she'll

deign to make an appearance today. And don't look at me like that. I just answer the phones. Reporters run on their own schedules, and I'm at their mercy."

I offered a commiserating nod. "Animals and a souffle stand control my schedule."

"Lunch is still my own," he said, shoving large dark-rimmed sunglasses over his eyes. "And I've got plans with a hot latte and a filthy romance novel. Good luck on your quest," he called, striding hurriedly away.

I looked in both directions, then headed for the nearest coffee shop, hoping not to run into the receptionist again. He'd probably assume I was a stalker.

Corner Cup sat on the corner of Main Street and River Drive, across from The Weathervane, a café I loved. The lines were long there, and I shot down a bolt of jealousy as I opened the coffee shop door. Sweet scents of caramel and vanilla filled my lungs as I got in line.

A woman I recognized as the shop's owner, Sally, waved when it was my turn at the counter. "Well, look at you, Miss Eggers. Don't you look lovely."

"Thank you, ma'am," I said. "You look nice as well." I smoothed my windswept hair from the four-mile bike ride and tried not to fuss with my clothing as well. The ankle-length dress I'd chosen this morning was white with a navy floral pattern and enough material to hide my legs when I pedaled. The garment easily earned five stars for practicality. Zero for aesthetic.

Sally wore a hairnet over a brown bob, and a logoed apron over her t-shirt and jeans. The look she gave me suggested she felt the same way about her outfit as I did mine. "Well, lookie here." Her gaze flicked to the pet carrier in my hand, and she leaned over the counter in our direction. "Hello, Thelma, sweet chicken. How are you today?"

Thelma clucked a series of soft complaints.

Sally beamed. Then, seeming to recall something unspoken, her attention snapped to the newspaper on her countertop. Yesterday's paper. With Wilhelmina's article facing up for all to see. "Oh," she said, swiping it out of sight. "Sorry about that. We were swamped earlier this week, so I've been trying to catch up on the news. Just one more day to go."

"It's fine. I'm in town looking for Wilhelmina. Any chance you've seen her?"

"Afraid not. That woman's never in one place more than ten minutes. You know, for what it's worth, I wouldn't worry about that article. Folks know how good your souffles are. They'll be back."

I pursed my lips and nodded. "Thanks."

"If I was you, I'd just ignore the whole thing and pretend it never happened. I've been telling everyone the only good thing that's come from that website is the optional texting app. That one I'd like to keep."

I frowned, unfamiliar. "There's an app?"

"Oh!" Her expression lit up. "There is, and you're going to love it. It uses a calendar to send reminders about sales and events. Once you sign up, you can follow as many stores as you want. I tell everyone who comes in here to register for those texts and notifications, then I blast Corner Cup news to all my subscribers. You could do the same!"

I blinked, considering. If I could send photos, I was certain images of the sunrise over the wildflower fields, with Souffle the Day in the backdrop, would make at least a few people want to give my place a try. "Thank you," I said, feeling slightly renewed. "I'm going to try that."

"Do it," she said. "You won't be disappointed."

I bought an iced sweet tea for me and a bottle of water for Thelma, then headed back into the day.

I stopped near my bicycle and set Thelma's crate on the ground. I poured a small amount of water into her collapsible bowl and slid the drink inside the carrier. "You'd better have a few sips before we get going again. July heat is no joke, and you don't want to get dehydrated."

Thelma sampled her drink, and I took a long pull on mine.

A woman tucked into the shadows at the coffee shop's edge caught my eye, and I waved. "Mrs. Carin?"

She smiled awkwardly, then inched in my direction, blue eyes fixed on the line outside her café across the street.

"What are you doing there?" I asked.

"I'm just taking a few minutes to breathe," she said. "It's been busy all morning, and I wasn't prepared." She flicked a finger in the direction of her shop. "The sales are nice. Don't get me wrong, but I needed a minute to recenter."

I tried my best not to be envious. "Feeling better?"

"A little," she said, casting a little wave toward Thelma's crate at my feet. "How are y'all? I saw that awful article in the paper and on Local Yum. It was all just ridiculous."

"Thanks." I did my best not to slouch or grimace. Was there anyone the unfavorable words about my café hadn't reached? "I'm hoping to run into Wilhelmina. I want to ask about her article, but she's proving tougher to track down than I expected. I might have to switch gears and ask Mr. Flint if he'll consider another visit instead. I'd like the chance to change his mind. Souffle the Day is perfectly lovely, even if the location isn't quite his style."

"Oh, hun." Her brows dipped, and her mouth formed a sad smile. "I hate that this has you so upset. I knew that town website was going to be trouble."

*Everyone could at least agree on that*, I thought. And given my current situation, I wasn't of a mind to argue.

"Well," Mrs. Carin sighed, glancing again at The Weathervane. "I should get back."

"Have a good day," I said, trying to be happy for her hoard

of customers, while I still had a mass of frozen souffle batter and an abundance of eggs going unused. "Mrs. Carin," I said, stopping her before she could walk away. "Any chance you could use some extra eggs? Mary and I will have more than we can use until business picks up again at the souffle stand."

A temporary deal with The Weathervane would please Mary and buy me time to sort things out. I didn't mind trading my eggs within the community again, but I wouldn't be able to buy Mary's without a way to use them.

Mrs. Carin nodded. "Bring them by when you can, and we'll pay the going rate. I'll let the staff know in case I'm not there when you stop by."

"Thank you."

"Louisa!" A familiar voice called, and the muscles of my shoulders tightened in response.

Mrs. Carin's eyes widened, and she made a soft choking sound before nearly stepping into traffic in her getaway.

Leaving me alone with Mama.

## CHAPTER THREE

"*D*arling," Mama said, working a white lace fan in front of her face and looking me over with critical eyes.

I touched my hair again, and she frowned.

Mama hated fidgeting.

She wore smart tan tailored dress pants, with a sleeveless cream blouse and pearl buttons. Her fawn pumps and camel-colored purse accented the crisp, flawless look. A delicate double gold chain hung across her exposed collarbone where the blouse cut into a modest V. "Generous of you to speak with the competition," she said, turning her eyes to Mrs. Carin's retreating form.

I wasn't surprised she'd steer clear of Mama, who tended to rub folks the wrong way, but it was a little odd Mama had bothered to mention her at all. Typically, she didn't bother to comment on many folks' existence. Even when they were right in front of her.

"Hi, Mama," I said, stepping forward to kiss her soft cheek. "It's nice to see you."

"Is it?" She glanced at Thelma's crate, then gazed at me

with a familiar mix of love and frustration. A look I likely returned. Mama and I were the same height when she wasn't in heels. Our faces both round and youthful, belying our ages to most. She pursed her small pink lips. "You're not an easy woman to get ahold of."

"I know. Cell signal is weak in Meadowbrook," I explained, not for the first time.

"You remember where I live?" she asked, daring me to claim otherwise, since I'd been raised there and it was only a few miles away. "If you're ever having trouble with your phone, feel free to drop by."

Mama inherited the property from her family who'd owned the same plot of land for nearly two-hundred years. The estate was grand and lavish, named Laurelwood at its founding, for the breathtaking scenery, including countless ancient trees and an abundance of mountain laurel. The home had maintained a full staff since the day it was built, though there was only Mama to serve now. A dozen or so acres were opened seasonally to the public as a small botanical garden and the county's only living-history museum.

Mama hosted Civil War reenactments and field trips, held fundraisers and fancy teas, all for charity, in an attempt to preserve the history of Cromwell and the legacy of our family. Managing and maintaining it all required another staff. And Mama led them as well. She was beloved, admired and feared in equal measures.

It terrified me to know I would be her one day.

"If it's so nice to see me," she said sweetly, "why not do it more often?"

"Sorry, Mama," I said, not exactly meaning it. But not *not* meaning it either. With Mama, everything was blurry and complicated.

"Do you have time for coffee?" she asked, pulling open the coffee shop door before I could say no.

I opened my mouth to say I already had an iced tea, but she plucked it from my hand and motioned me inside.

"I'll get you a fresh drink."

I sighed and lifted Thelma's crate, then watched helplessly as Mama dropped my cup into the trash and got in line to order.

She purchased two skinny lattes, without asking what I wanted, then chose a round table for two near the big shop window. A place where she could both see and be seen. Two of her gold medal sports.

I set Thelma's crate on the floor at my feet.

Mama crossed her legs and fixed me with a concerned stare. "I read the review of your souffle stand on the Local Yum last night. And the *Chronicle's* recap."

I shifted unintentionally, and her eyes narrowed.

"How are you holding up?"

"I'm looking for Wilhelmina now," I said, placing my hands in my lap where she couldn't see me fidget. "And I'm willing to speak with Mr. Flint as well. I'm sure I can get one of them to revisit the subject."

"Good. It's important to take charge and know your worth. Don't let either of them dismiss your request if they try. In this situation your youth and beauty will be disadvantages. You'll likely be seen as a child or stupid. Or both. It feels like an incredible burden to carry now, especially having started your own business, but wait until you're clearly over forty. Then people your current age will treat you as if you're decrepit or stupid. Or both. What matters is that you set them straight. Be kind but direct. And always firm."

"We Eggers women will not be dismissed," I said, finishing a pep talk I'd heard before. The first time I'd gotten the speech, I was in elementary school and Billy Myers told me it was dress-up day before flipping my skirt up to show the class my cartoon-print underpants. I'd punched him in the nose and been given detention. Mama gave me the talk, then handed me her telephone. I called the principal to request a meeting with him, Billy and Billy's parents. Mama attended for moral support, and I delivered the information she'd given me over ice cream the night before. What Billy had done was sexual harassment and bullying. He'd taunted me. Then touched me without my permission and willfully caused me humiliation and duress. I would file charges against him and his parents unless Billy was punished and instructed to never again touch a woman without consent. If the school didn't punish him, I would register a grievance with the board.

Billy ate lunch alone the rest of the week and never told another girl it was dress-up day.

Mama's expression turned prideful. "Very good. Now, onto our next order of business."

I sipped my coffee, appreciating the taste of my former life. I hadn't had a skinny latte in three years. "What's that?"

"The season is in full swing for the gardens and museum. Both have extended hours through the end of next month, and we need more knowledgeable, skilled hands on deck. More actors who know the drill and more backstage support for the next few months. You know this better than anyone else. You've filled every role from butter churner to business accountant to marketing rep at one point or another. You have a lifetime of experience, a pedigree that makes lesser pedigrees shrink in fear and an impressive education. What do you say?"

"Thank you?" I asked, avoiding the real question.

"Funny," she said. "So, what will it be? You can pick any position you'd like."

I counted silently to ten before answering in my sweetest, most southern of voices. "I'm afraid I can't help you this season, Mama. As you mentioned, I have a new small business to run, and it takes a lot of my time. Not to mention the maintenance and care of my hens and donkeys. And the trouble I'm attempting to work through following those unflattering articles."

Mama stared, expression flat, but pleasant, in case anyone was looking.

I chewed my bottom lip and kneaded my hands beneath the table. "I'm also planning a wedding," I added hastily.

Mama's eyes widened. "A wedding?" Her gaze dropped in search of my ring finger, then flipped back to meet my hot-cheeked stare. "Whose wedding? You haven't agreed to marry someone from that commune of yours, have you? Is it that big Scot."

I frowned. "No, Mama. I'm not getting married. I'm planning a wedding." *For donkeys*, I omitted. *Assuming Jill says yes.* "What big Scot?"

She rolled her eyes, slow and dramatic as she kicked back to uncross, then recross her legs. "The giant ginger who's always popping up around you looking like that *Outlander* fellow."

"Eli?" I asked, stumped by the fact Mama knew he existed and that she thought he followed me. But he did look a little like the actor she'd mentioned, not that I'd agree with her out loud. "Eli is Irish."

"Hmm." She looked me over again, the wheels of her mind clearly turning. "Why can't he help with your chores and animals while you help me at Laurelwood? Like it or not, it will all be yours one day. I've no one else to leave it to, and I won't live forever."

"You're forty-six," I said blandly. "I think you've got a couple good weeks left in you."

Her lips twitched, fighting one of her rare but breath-taking smiles. "Better to come home and accept your rightful role now than later when I'm gone and you're grieving," she said. "Besides, what will Nana Hams say when she visits again and you're still living in Meadowbrook?"

Nana Hams was Mama's aunt. She lived in New Orleans and bullied folks there, like Mama did here. Though, instead of a massive living museum, Nana Hams had a group of historic plantation owners and a pack of trained llamas. The Llama Mamas competed with some other group of elite hen owners to see who could raise more charity money at various events in the city. I'd been to Nana Hams's estate many times, and I dearly loved New Orleans, but I didn't want to live anywhere that competition was a lifestyle. "I live in Meadowbrook. It's part of the same town. There's nothing wrong with living apart from you, especially at my age. Plus I'm happy," I snapped.

Mama raised a pointed brow, and I sat taller.

"Sorry," I said more quietly. "I'm happy to help, if I can, but I'll need to make arrangements on my end and fix this issue with my souffle stand before I can do anything else. My animals and my business are the priority right now. They count on me to be there."

"Fine," she said, lowering the judgmental brow. "Set your house in order, then come over for tea and we'll discuss the details of your assistance at Laurelwood. If you aren't able to resurrect your business after this debacle, it could be a sign."

"It's not a debacle or a sign," I said, checking my watch, then standing. I'd completely lost track of time and probably missed Wilhelmina again, if she'd even stopped at the newspaper. "This is all just a misunderstanding. Besides, if I can't save my business, it will mean I failed. And Eggerses don't fail."

She sighed. "All right."

"Goodbye, Mama." I kissed her cheek, lifted Thelma's crate, then walked calmly through the door.

I squinted on the sidewalk, allowing my eyes to adjust to the light. Mama watched from her seat at the window inside.

The flicker of determination to succeed grew brighter as I marched toward the rack where I'd left my bike.

"Let's stop at the park next," I said. "We'll stretch your wings for a few minutes, then try the newspaper again. If Wilhelmina isn't there, we'll look for Mr. Flint, then double back to the paper. And we aren't going home until we talk to one of them."

As if on cue, the light at the corner changed, and Wilhelmina drove by, her historic truck pointed away from town.

"Dang it."

CHAPTER FOUR

*N*inety minutes later, Thelma and I had struck out on all counts. We hadn't located Mr. Flint, and Wilhelmina hadn't returned. So, we headed home to regroup and make a better plan.

An unusual number of cars moved in our direction as well.

And they all made the turn toward Meadowbrook.

"What on earth?" I mumbled, pedaling faster.

*Bawk-ah!*

Clearly Thelma noticed the oddity too.

Why were all these people visiting our community? What had happened while we were away? And why did it matter to so many townies?

A car was slowing to take the gently pitted road. The world darkened as we entered the forest, then brightened as the dense canopy of tree limbs allowed the sun to shine through. I left the earthen road and whizzed passed a line of parked vehicles that led all the way to my souffle stand.

I nearly dropped my bike as I dismounted.

People ate on picnic benches in the pasture, stood in clusters near the open doors and waited in a long line at the counter.

Mary frowned as she attempted to make change while clutching a mixing bowl to her middle.

"Do you see this?" I asked Thelma as I unfastened her crate.

*Bawk-ah!*

I bent to set her free in the grass.

Was Mary so desperate to sell her eggs that she'd wait for me to leave, then reopen my café for the day? And if so, how had she gotten so many people to come?

I darted toward the counter. "What's going on here?" I whisper-hissed as Mary passed the next person in line a tray with two quiches and two coffees.

"I don't know," she said, expression turning mildly frantic. "Flint came here looking for you, and I didn't want him to leave until you gave him the solid lashing he deserves, so I opened the shop and told him you'd be right back. Other people started showing up after that. Even Wilhelmina."

My eyes widened as I scanned the crowd, locating both the octogenarian reporter and the critic in question, thankfully on two different sides of the crowd.

"I ran out of the souffle batter in the freezer," Mary said, "So I started making quiches. There's no way I could replicate your souffles."

"Good thinking. And thank you. Has Flint eaten anything, or has he just sat there checking his watch?"

"I think he's waiting for you. He didn't order." She wiped her hands on her apron and moved back to the register as another pair of customers approached.

The oven timer dinged, and I saw an opportunity. "I'll be right back," I said, grabbing a tray and warm quiche.

I arranged the delicious-smelling dish alongside a carafe

and mug of fresh coffee, then lifted my chin and headed in Flint's direction.

"Go get him," Mary called.

Wilhelmina and several others took notice and quieted to watch me on my mission.

Mr. Flint stood when I arrived.

"Hello," I said, sliding the tray onto his table. "I'm so glad you came back. I was just in town looking for you. Please give my work another try," I said, infusing the request with a sweet but firm tone. "This is a mushroom, mozzarella and onion quiche. Maybe you'll prefer this to the souffle."

"Of course," he said. Wind ruffled his thick dark hair, which was combed neatly in the style of most seven-year-old boys. He tugged on the thighs of his khakis as he retook his seat and motioned me to join him.

"Thank you." I sat on a deep exhale.

The afternoon had taken an unexpected, but lovely turn, and I smiled.

"Ms. Eggers," he said. "I appreciate your willingness to speak with me. I'm not sure I'd be as kind, were the tables turned." The wind picked up, beating the material of his short-sleeved plaid button up against his narrow frame.

Still smiling, I nodded toward the quiche. "I'd really appreciate it if you'd try it. I didn't make this one, Mary did," I said, hooking a thumb in the direction of my friend. "But she's pretty good in the kitchen, and this is really what folks should come here for." I motioned to the beautiful scenery and crowd of mingling townies and Meadowbrookers. "It's nice, right?"

He nodded patiently, then lifted the fork and took a bite, still nodding as he chewed and swallowed. "Very nice," he said, following the bite with a sip of coffee.

"Would you like cream?" I asked.

He raised a flat palm in my direction. "No, thank you. I really just want to clear the air."

I stared at the quiche and waited while he took another bite. If only he'd thought my souffle was very nice. And hadn't made a negative public review of my fledgling business. "Mr. Flint," I said, feeling the fire from Mama's pep talk return. "I believe your assessment of my food and this place was unfair, and I'd like you to post a follow-up review. Maybe this time you can try more than one item from the menu and spend a little time talking to other guests. This might not be your favorite spot, but Souffle the Day is reuniting Cromwell with its love of farm-to-fork foods and outdoor atmosphere. One dish at a time."

His face reddened, and I feared a public rebuttal was on the way.

My muscles tensed. What would Mama do?

I looked to Mary for support and found her, along with most of the others present, staring.

Wilhelmina had moved closer and lifted a cell phone in our direction, presumably recording the interaction so she could report on it.

A hot-pink handbag with fuzzy yellow pompom tassels caught my eye, and I hoped one of Mama's friends wasn't here. Mama and her ladies all loved that particular designer.

I turned back to Mr. Flint.

He set his fork aside, clearly no longer enjoying the meal. "What's in this dish?" he asked, the words cracking out of him like gunfire.

"Eggs," I stammered, stunned by his sudden rage. "Cheese, mushrooms and onions." I frowned as his face grew redder. "I called it a mushroom, mozzarella and onion quiche when I gave it to you." Surely if he didn't like one of those ingredients, he would've said so.

Was all this drama for show? Did he want half the town to hear him bully me?

Suspicion needled me, and I wondered if I was being provoked for something my mama had done.

"Cream?" he asked, tugging his collar and loosening his tie.

"I'm not sure," I admitted. I typically didn't add cream, but Mary might. "If so, I assure you it's as organic as everything else. You can even meet the cows who contributed if you stop at the Thompsons's cottage on your way out."

I tipped my chin up, darting my attention through the waiting crowd, as if to say, I know my stuff and it's all good stuff.

"Ms. Eggers," he said, the words tighter than before. "I'm not complaining. I just wanted to clarify." He cleared his throat. Twice. "As for the article, I want to speak with you about that."

I tensed. "I still can't believe you wrote it. My business suffered as a result." Though, it probably didn't appear that way to him at the moment. I glanced around, still unsure why so many people had arrived out of the blue.

My phone rang, and I glanced away to silence it.

Mama was calling, as if she somehow knew I was losing my nerve.

"If you don't like my cooking or the enchanting and peaceful setting of this eatery, that's fine. It's your opinion and you're entitled to it," I continued. "But frankly, it's just bad manners to yuck someone else's yum. And a lot of people like it here."

He raised his hand to silence me as someone called my name.

Eli moved swiftly in my direction, apparently alarmed by the crowd that had encircled us. "Louisa?"

"It's f—," I said, cut off by Mr. Flint's reaching hand.

He tipped forward, clutching the neckline of my dress and dragging me to the ground.

"Mr. Flint!" I screamed. "Stop!"

The crowd broke into a clamor of voices as I struggled to get him off of me.

The older man vanished, and Eli appeared, having tossed him aside by the back of his shirt.

"Goodness!" I gasped, accepting his hand to pull me upright.

Eli drew me against him protectively, speaking into my ear as we turned to Mr. Flint for an explanation. "Are you okay?"

"I think so. I don't know why he did that." My voice cracked as the violation registered fully. He'd tackled me without warning.

A woman's voice broke the sudden silence, and she fell to her knees at my assailant's side. "I don't think he's breathing!"

"What?" I stepped away from Eli for a better look at Mr. Flint's unnaturally red and splotchy face.

"He's having a heart attack!" someone yelled. "Call an ambulance!"

Eli raised his phone to one ear, tugging me back a step. "I'm no medic, but that looks like anaphylaxis to me."

# CHAPTER FIVE

"I can't believe you killed him," Mary said, climbing onto the picnic table beside me and resting her booted feet on the seat. The length of her deep purple skirt fell over the boots' laces. "I only wanted you to tell him off. You always take things too far."

I grimaced. "I didn't kill him. He just fell over dead."

"That's going to be a tough story to sell. Especially since you were in the middle of delivering a sound verbal lashing. I guess words really are weapons."

"You told me to set him straight," I said, chewing my nails and entertaining her dark dialogue to keep me from crying again. As long as we were talking about it so plainly, it wasn't real. And just maybe he wasn't dead at all. Maybe he'd had a heart attack and his pulse was too weak to be found by a lay person. Maybe the paramedics would soon set everyone straight.

"Well, when I said go get him," she continued. "I didn't think you'd literally. Get. Him."

I watched red and white lights cut through the sky as emergency responders worked on Mr. Flint and spoke with the remaining crowd. Most folks had left the moment someone screamed for an ambulance.

Eli moved back in our direction, head shaking upon approach. He took his place at my opposite side and set a palm on my back, apparently prepared to play angel to Mary's devil. "Louisa didn't kill him, and it wasn't a heart attack, but he is dead. I just overheard a medic summon the coroner."

"A coroner?" Mary said, leaning forward to see around me. "Why not just take him to the hospital morgue?"

Eli glanced at me before answering. "I still think this was anaphylaxis. The coroner will make an initial evaluation here to preserve the potential crime scene."

I pinched my bottom lip between my thumb and first finger, all attempts at holding back the tears were futile. Mr. Flint was dead. And I'd been yelling at him when he died.

My stomach flopped, and I wrapped an arm around my middle. "He asked what was in the quiche."

Eli turned to me. "Today?"

I nodded.

Mary gasped. "Wait. Does that mean I killed him?"

"Stop saying anyone killed him," I whispered. "No one will ever eat here again."

I felt a pang of shame at the thought. A man had died. I shouldn't be thinking of myself, or the café, at a time like this.

But what if I had to move back to Laurelwood and live with Mama?

Sweat formed on the back of my neck.

Cromwell's entire police force was on the scene. All three members. They'd divided duties. One interviewing the crowd. One scanning the larger scene and now flagging Mr. Flint's cup, fork and plate. The third kept watch on the perimeter, scanning me from time to time.

The coroner arrived minutes later and began a battery of tasks, like cleaning under Mr. Flint's fingernails.

He'd scratched me on his way down, so I supposed they'd find my DNA there.

I let my head fall forward into waiting palms. This day had been awful on every single level. I was a dedicated silver-lining gal, but currently I didn't know what to be most upset about. *Besides his death*, I thought, kicking myself internally again.

Souffle the Day was surely ruined. My reputation would forever be marred with flashing red lights after this. And Mama was going to lose her mind.

At least I was alive, I guessed. Mr. Flint certainly had it worse.

Wilhelmina's voice met my ear on the breeze, and I raised my head to search for her. She handed her giant cell phone to an officer. "I got it all on tape," she declared, drawing a second officer to her side. The trio closed ranks around the device, watching intently for several seconds before raising their eyes to me.

I whispered a tiny swear word.

"What did you say?" Mary asked, twisting on the table beside me to stare in mock horror. "Why, Louisa Eggers, bless your soul. I didn't think you knew that word."

"I don't," I said. "And you didn't hear it."

"I absolutely did," she said, swinging her attention to Eli. "Did you know this little flower is not what she seems?"

"Most people aren't," he said, eyes distant and lips downturned.

Mary cupped a hand around her mouth and leaned toward my ear. "He isn't either."

Eli's standard frown grew more severe, and he turned hard hazel eyes on her.

She beamed, having successfully created more drama where there was already enough for a lifetime.

Meanwhile, Cromwell's only female officer approached, scrutinizing Eli, Mary and me as if we were specimens of fungus in a lab. "Louisa," she said. "Eli. Mary."

We'd all become acquainted recently when my ex-boyfriend was murdered. Local police hadn't exactly proven themselves to be gold medal detectives that time. And I feared this could be a repeat performance.

"Officer Anthony," I said.

Behind her, the younger of the two male officers took photos of, then bagged the remainder of Mr. Flint's quiche and coffee, his plate and fork.

"I need to get your statements about what happened here as you recall it," she said, keen blue eyes fixed on me. "Maybe start with why the souffle stand is open for the first time after eleven A.M. Was there a reason behind the impromptu timeline?"

I took a steadying breath and called upon years of debutante training, then told the details of the last few hours from my perspective.

The officer took notes in a small spiral notebook like cops used on T.V.

Eli pressed his hands to his hips. "What's the coroner thinking was the cause?"

She glanced over her shoulder, expression solemn. "Right now? Anaphylaxis. That could change after the autopsy."

My stomach churned at the word autopsy.

Eli rubbed his beard. He'd called it. And I wondered how he'd known.

Did Eli have a deadly allergy? Had he known someone who'd died similarly?

"Mr. Flint asked me what was in the quiche," I said softly. "I thought he was being arrogant. Complaining. Maybe even making a scene for all the onlookers."

Officer Anthony jotted something down and closed her book. "He was probably complaining that he felt as if he was dying and trying to figure out why."

"He's eaten here before and was fine," I said. "All my dishes are comprised of roughly the same ingredients. Eggs from Meadowbrook hens. Cream, milk and butter from the Thompsons's cows, and chopped veggies from our gardens."

Compassion fell from her features and her expression tightened. "I read the review."

I let my eyes shut for one long beat, hoping I'd imagined the accusation in her tone. When I opened my eyes, I pleaded my case. "The quiche he ate wasn't even meant for him specifically. I took it from the oven without asking first."

"Who was the quiche meant for?" she asked, interest piqued.

Mary raised her hand, pulling Officer Anthony's eyes her way. "I was cooking and taking orders. I made the mozzarella, mushroom and onion dish for myself in the handful of moments when everyone else had been served and no one was in line. I planned to nibble on it between customers."

"She wouldn't poison herself," I said, relieved there wasn't any way for local police to presume I'd poisoned him with the meal.

Eli leaned closer, the way he always seemed to do when I was in distress. "Does Mr. Flint have any allergies? Could the reaction have been to something else? Maybe a bee sting?"

"That's what we intend to find out," Officer Anthony said. "Thank you for your time." She stepped back, eyes still on mine. "I'll be in touch."

I nodded.

EMTs helped the coroner load Mr. Flint into a white panel van.

Police Chief Mertz and his dopey, gangly son, also known

as Officer Mark Mertz headed toward us next.

Mark had gotten on my last nerve since elementary school, and I didn't predict a change. I was shocked when I learned he'd followed his father's footsteps into law enforcement, though I suspected spineless people enjoyed having some measure of power. And also that his dad hadn't given him a choice.

Chief Mertz locked his thumbs behind a belt nearly hidden under his belly and stared. "Coroner's going to pull the contents of Flint's stomach and see what he can find."

"Gross," Mary complained.

"It'll be a day or two before the autopsy is complete."

The spectators murmured, gazing woefully at their empty plates and cups, then me and the souffle stand.

"My food isn't poisoned," I called to them.

They hurried toward their cars.

"This isn't what it seems," I said, continuing to project my voice. "I'll figure it out. Then you can come back."

The chief shook his head. "I don't think so, Ms. Eggers. Your souffle stand is officially closed until further notice."

## CHAPTER SIX

*I* curled on the window seat in my cottage's small sunroom the next morning. The converted porch space overlooking my side yard had become my favorite place to read in the rain or watch the stars in the winter. As a bonus, it was easy to keep an eye on Thelma while staying out of the relentless midday sun. Also a prime location for tea drinking and pondering my life choices. Normally those choices involved chores, hobbies and what I'd make for dinner.

At the moment, all I could think about was Mr. Flint's dying body dragging mine to the ground.

Mary appeared on the sidewalk a moment later, a basket of eggs on her arm. She spotted me in the sunroom and changed directions, opening the screen door at my side. "You look horrible."

"Thank you," I said, swinging my feet onto the floor. "I feel like I look." I upturned an empty cup on my tea tray. I'd brought an extra, suspecting someone would be around soon enough to check on me. Without the souffle stand to open,

I'd had nothing to do with my time following morning chores.

Mary set the basket on a table stacked with books, then flopped into an armchair and accepted the tea when I poured. "This is miserable," she said. "First Flint criticizes Souffle the Day and ruins business. Then he comes back uninvited and unannounced, brings a crowd, and dies. On video. Now I'm out of a job. What am I supposed to do with all my eggs?"

I gripped the tightening muscles along the back of my neck and across my shoulders. "The stand's closure is only temporary. Obviously I didn't poison him. We just have to be patient and trust the coroner to see our food and drink weren't tainted. Meanwhile, I've spoken to Mrs. Carin at The Weathervane about taking more of your eggs."

"Good," Mary said. "Thank you. But what if you're wrong about your shop? What if he gave someone else a bad review and they followed him here to make sure he never gave another one?"

I grimaced. "First of all, yikes. You're talking about intentional, premeditated murder. Second of all, I took that quiche straight from the oven. No one else touched it after you put it in to cook, and since it was meant for you, it's safe to assume you didn't poison it."

Mary listened attentively, her frown fixed in place.

"He wasn't poisoned," I said. "Not with our food. So, we just have to wait for the coroner's report to clear things up. Then this will all be fine."

"You keep saying that, but nothing about this is fine," she griped. "Your reputation is ruined, and I need money. I have to sell my eggs, or find buyers for my hens, because I need an income to keep them safe, fed and housed. You have to fix this."

"Me?" I squeaked. "How am I supposed to fix this?" I was

still reeling over her accusation that my reputation was ruined. Mary tended toward doom and gloom, but if she was right, I was in massive trouble. I'd invested my savings in that café. Worse, I'd dipped into my trust, which put me in debt to my mama. I had no doubt she knew exactly how much I'd withdrawn and the reason I'd needed it.

Mama knew, heard and saw everything. Especially where I was concerned.

Mary drained her tea and set the empty cup back onto the tray with a clatter. "I don't know. Work your magic. Call your mother. Find the real killer. I don't care what you do. Just do— something."

"I'm not calling my mama. That's an absolute no. And I don't have any magic, so there go all your ideas."

My front doorbell rang, and I shoved onto my feet, leaving the cozy pillow nook behind.

"Not all my ideas," she said.

I shuffled past the white wrought iron tea cart and into my cottage living area. The decor was an eclectic mix of things I'd brought from home, things I'd gotten in trade for eggs, souffles and hens, and items collected from thrift stores. The bright, whimsical color palette made me happy, as did the shabby chic style. I'd arranged handmade pieces from local artists beside antique trimmings from Cromwell's history to create a quirky and inviting space uniquely mine. Given the fact I had barely over one thousand square feet to keep and display it all, my cottage could also be described as a bit cluttered.

I opened the door with a smile.

Eli looked shyly back, and my ridiculous heart skipped a beat.

I'd had a crush on him for more than a year. Aside from always being ready to help anyone who needed a hand, he was amazingly kind and ridiculously gorgeous. He also had big, rough hands, and I appreciated the way he wielded an ax to chop wood.

His faint Irish accent was icing on the beefcake.

"Morning," he said, spinning a black ball cap in his hand. "I thought I should drop by and check on you. After everything that happened yesterday," he clarified.

"Oh, thank you," I said, face heating furiously, as it always did in his presence.

I dragged my eyes away from his big, rough, handy hands and smiled. "Come in."

I turned toward the sunroom and tried to pull myself together. "Mary's here. We were just having tea. Would you like some?"

"Can I trouble you for a glass of ice water?" He rubbed a forearm over his brow, and I pressed a palm to my collarbone. "I've been chopping and stacking firewood all morning."

*My stars in heaven.*

"Mm hmm," I said, changing directions at the request, forcing images of him chopping and stacking wood from my mind. It was a show that never disappointed. "Be right back," I called over my shoulder. "Mary's in the sunroom. Y'all go on and visit."

I stopped at the refrigerator and rested my forehead on the cool metal, taking a minute to remind myself I was twenty-six. Not sixteen. Yes, I loved imagining what it would feel like to lie next to Eli on a soft wool picnic blanket under the apple tree, laughing over inside jokes and feeding one another strawberries picked from the fields. And maybe stealing kisses behind his big straw hat, while amused neighbors shook their heads, elated for us, because we'd fallen in love. And sure, sometimes I imagined what his calloused palms would feel like skimming over the delicate curves of my bare skin, but darn it, a woman should be allowed to have her fantasies without feeling guilty or lighting up like a bright red traffic light. "Shape up, Eggers," I chided myself softly.

"Everything okay?" Eli asked.

I spun in place and blinked at his unexpected appearance in the kitchen archway. "Perfect," I said, feeling the heat in my cheeks once more.

I yanked open the appliance door hard enough to tear it off the hinges and nearly dislocated my arm in the process. "You?" I freed the pitcher of cold water and filled a glass from the cupboard. "Here you are." I set the glass on my island, careful not to slosh the contents over the rim.

I put the pitcher away and closed the refrigerator with extra care.

"You sure? Cause you seem a little jazzed up," he said, lifting the glass to his lips.

I took a seat at the table, certain I was losing my mind.

Eli downed the water, then set the glass aside. "I thought you might be like this today. It's okay to feel overwhelmed you know?"

I released a slow, easy breath. "Really? Because nothing about how I feel seems right."

"A man died in front of you last night," he said. "He fell on you. That's pretty traumatic."

I nodded.

"How'd you sleep?"

"I didn't sleep," I admitted, thankful Eli had assumed one-hundred percent of my erratic behavior was a result of the recent trauma.

"You should've called," he said softly. His voice soothed like warm honey. "I would've come over and kept you company."

Mary moseyed into the cramped kitchen and looked from me to Eli, then back. "You could've called me too."

"Thank you," I said, swinging my attention from friend to friend. "Both of you. I passed the time by researching Mr. Flint. I looked him up online and read his other reviews on the village website."

Eli's hazel eyes flashed, then narrowed. "Why were you doing that?"

I shrugged. "It's what I did when Ben died unexpectedly. It seemed like the thing to do again."

"Ben was murdered," Eli said. "Mr. Flint had an allergic reaction."

I chewed my lip, and Eli leveled me with a no nonsense stare, setting his palms on the table before me.

"We've talked about this before," he said, voice harder than I was accustomed to hearing it. "You said you wouldn't launch anymore private investigations. Not after what happened last time."

"Hey now," Mary said. "Not to make this about me, but I believe I was the one nearly killed."

I fought a grin. She'd had a concussion, but I supposed the blow to the head could've been deadly. Thankfully she'd survived to become my closest friend. "I just wanted to know something about Mr. Flint. Like you said. He died right in front of me."

Eli straightened and crossed his arms. "What did you want to know?"

I looked at my nails, then Mary, who tented her brows as if she was waiting for the answer too. "I wondered if I'd find evidence of anyone who might've wanted to hurt him, and if that person had somehow used my souffle stand to accomplish the goal. I also looked up the top ten reasons people kill."

Mary slid her gaze to Eli.

"Louisa." He slumped onto the chair across from me. "That isn't healthy."

I leaned forward, matching his posture. Forearms on the table, hands clasped. "Everything I read seemed to say murder boils down to three things. Money, revenge or pride, and even those motives are often one and the same."

Mary pulled a stool away from the island and sat at the end of the table. "Mr. Flint wasn't wealthy, and his job was pretty unimpressive. So, I can't see money or pride as the objective. Did he even get paid to do those reviews?"

"I don't know," I said. "But I learned he was married."

She wrinkled her nose. "Really?"

"Yeah." I nodded. "And about three months ago, she cut him out of all her social media posts. She stopped sharing images with him in them. Stopped tagging him in memes. Just stopped acknowledging his existence."

"Ohhh," Mary cooed, pinning an elbow to her thigh and setting her chin in her upturned hand. "That's interesting. Tell me more."

I swiveled on my seat to face her. "Three weeks ago, she changed her relationship status from married to single, but there haven't been any divorce papers filed with the county."

Eli groaned. "You checked the public records?"

"Yes." They were all available online. "And," I said, "Mr. Flint wasn't the man who started the Local Yum column. It was another guy named Dirk Yoder. Flint took over shortly after Dirk's initial round of reviews."

Mary opened her mouth, then shut it. "That would certainly hurt my pride."

I nodded. "That's what I thought. Unless the first guy chose to step down for some reason, which is possible."

"Flint definitely wasn't a professional writer," Mary said. "His article was a mess. Poor prose. Too short. Not a lot about the actual food. It was actually pretty weird. Aren't those posts vetted?"

"I'm not sure about the vetting, but I read a few of his

other reviews, and they weren't like the one he wrote for Souffle the Day," I said. "Something was probably going on at the time he wrote it. Maybe he was rushing to meet a deadline?" *Or maybe*, I hoped, *whatever killed him was already taking hold the day before.*

"Interesting." Mary tapped a fingertip to her lips.

"No," Eli said. "It's not interesting. It's wrong to dig into a man's life now that he's dead, unless you're a member of law enforcement trying to find his killer. You are not law enforcement. In fact, you're probably the main suspect right now."

"Ugh." Mary slid onto her feet and returned my stool to the island. "You're such a drag," she told Eli. "I have chores. Call me when he leaves." She pointed at his head, then saw herself out.

Eli's attention stayed on me while Mary made her exit. "Remember what happened last time," he said. "I'm not saying something so unthinkable will happen again, but it could, and I don't want you to get hurt. I think the best thing you can do right now is spend this time off work recovering from the shock of Flint's death and planning ways to rebuild your shop's reputation. Maybe work on that donkey wedding." He stood and sighed. "I've got to get going, but think about it, okay. You have plenty to do while the police deal with Flint's murder."

"You heard about the donkey wedding?" I asked, rising to walk him to the door.

He dipped his chin. "Mary told the Shoemakers, and they mentioned it when placing their order for firewood. They think it's a nice idea. A little strange, but I know you like to throw a party, and you love those donkeys."

"I really do. Will you come?"

He snorted. "Of course." He turned at the door and looked down at me. "In case you haven't noticed, when

## CHAPTER SEVEN

*D*onkey wedding plans were taking shape by lunch.

All my chores were finished, and I had loads of anxious energy to burn. I grabbed Thelma and my bicycle for another ride into town. Eli had been right about one thing. Sitting at home searching the internet for information on Mr. Flint wasn't helpful.

I needed to ask questions and talk to the people who had answers.

And I needed to order a few things for Jack and Jill's wedding. I was almost certain she planned to say yes.

*Bawk-ah!* Thelma complained as I hit a rough patch of road.

"Sorry."

The temperature was sweltering as we glided toward town, but the breeze created when coasting down hills was exhilarating.

Cromwell was inarguably one of the most beautiful places on earth, and everyone who lived here knew it. We had easy river access for white water rafting and fishing, boating and water skiing. An abundance of creeks made for great wading and the multitude of waterfalls would steal any nature-lover's breath.

The plethora of hiking trails, biking trails and rocky mountain faces made the landscape a virtual playground.

Our downtown area was a little light on shops and foot traffic, but that was probably only because everyone was busy enjoying the wilds.

I angled my bike onto the sidewalk and slowed at the nearest rack, then locked it up and unfastened Thelma's crate.

"First stop, the newspaper offices," I said. Hopefully we'd have more luck there today.

Wilhelmina came into view a moment later, standing outside The Pretty Pantry. She wore a bright-pink t-shirt tucked into elastic-waisted jeans with white orthopedic sneakers. Her extra-large sunglasses had white frames to match her shoes and hair.

She froze when she noticed me.

I forced an inviting smile, then picked up my pace.

Jeanie, the woman she'd been speaking with, fell silent as well, and the pair watched my approach.

"Hello," I called, offering a small wave.

Only Jeanie waved back. She was a few years older than me and infinitely more pleasant without trying. I appreciated her energy and passion as much as her kindness. Jeanie loved organization the way I loved eggs.

Her containers had changed my life when I'd lived at Laurelwood, with a bedroom closet the size of my current home. I'd left most of the racks, boxes and space savers at Mama's house, because there wasn't much space to save at the cottage. The strategy there was to pare down.

"I hope I'm not interrupting," I said, clutching Thelma's crate to my middle like a shield. As if her clucks and feathers could protect me from whatever might be said. Wilhelmina had been present while I'd yelled at a dying man, after all. And she'd filmed it. From her vantage, Flint's death probably seemed like anything but food poisoning. I wondered if she'd heard the theory.

"Not at all," Jeanie said, stepping back to welcome me into their little chat. "It's good to see you. Hi, Thelma!"

Thelma clucked steadily back, likely asking Jeanie about her mama, which was the proper southern response.

Jeanie's curly brown hair bobbed in the high ponytail where she'd wrangled it. Her brown eyes and dual dimples flashed with delight. "We were just discussing Cromwell's next community event. This new village website has been a real kick, right? Finally folks are starting to come together and mingle again. All my life, we've been moving away from one another, into the wilderness for alone time with nature or our closest friends. That's great and all, but what happened to building bonds with our neighbors and expanding our circles? Maybe even a little networking like they talk about on the internet and T.V."

"That's one of my favorite things about Meadowbrook," I said. "We all love and appreciate nature's beauty, but the human connection is just as important."

Jeanie nodded enthusiastically. "Exactly. We were just saying a street party would be a great way to bring folks downtown. We could set up barriers at either end of these two blocks, arrange displays on the sidewalks, get some music going, maybe sell refreshments. Games for kids. The whole kit and kaboodle. Maybe then folks would remember there are some shops in this town. Good ones."

"Sounds fun. Count me in," I said, daring a look in Wilhelmina's direction.

She eyed me cautiously.

"I'm glad you're here," I told the older woman. "I was actually looking for you. I wanted to thank you for not uploading that video to the new website or printing an article about what happened in the paper today."

My morning paper had arrived shortly after Eli and Mary left, and the notice in the crime section about Mr. Flint's death had been brief. I wasn't sure if that was Wilhelmina's choice or if my luck was improving. Either way, I was glad.

Jeanie grimaced and tipped her head over one shoulder. "I was so sorry I didn't stay last night. I wanted to be sure you were okay, but it didn't seem right to stick around with an ambulance on the way. I heard the rest of the story later. I'm glad you're doing fine. I'd probably be curled up in bed for a week after that. Your mama must be beside herself."

My shoulders tensed at her words. Should I be at home? Too upset to ask questions? When people saw me chatting and smiling, would they assume I was heartless? Unaffected? Guilty?

"Mama is shaken." She'd heard all about what happened and called a number of times since last night. I hadn't persuaded myself to answer yet. There was still too much to process, and talking with her about this would only get me wound up. But she'd left messages.

Another thing occurred to me as I contemplated Mama, thankful she hadn't been present for Flint's death. "I didn't know you were there," I said, lifting my eyes to Jeanie's. "I'm sorry you had to see that."

She patted my arm, then looked back to Wilhelmina. "Last night is a perfect example of how powerful the new text notification system is. Folks got notice about the upcoming event and Meadowbrook was swamped in under an hour."

"What event?" I asked before Wilhelmina could respond.

Jeanie looked to Wilhelmina.

I considered that a moment. "Y'all got text notifications?"

"Yes. Most of the town seemed to." Jeanie nodded.

Wilhelmina slid her eyes my way. "I got a message through the paper's tip line first. I motored right over there because I was trying to sort the whole thing. Frank was uncharacteristically negative in his review, which was why I covered it in the paper when he didn't return my call. The editor wants me to do more pieces on controversial topics. He thinks tension will sell papers." She looked briefly away, possibly feeling guilty for having added to my business troubles. "I wouldn't have been so curt in my recap if I'd had any idea this would happen. By the time I saw the text notification I was already en route."

"What did the text say?" I asked. "What made everyone stop what they were doing and show up?"

Jeanie still hadn't told me what event she'd referenced.

She pulled her phone from her pocket and looked at the screen. "Hang on. I think I've still got it."

I glanced around, strangely uncomfortable. It might've been paranoia, or embarrassment, discussing such unsavory things as a man's untimely death and previously poor behavior, on the sidewalk in broad daylight. But it felt as if I was being watched. Or maybe Mama was nearby. Her scrutiny always gave me chills.

"Got it," Jeanie said. She turned her phone screen to me.

I read the words aloud. "Showdown at Souffle the Day. Flint v. Eggers. Townie v. Hipster. Happening Now."

"It seems silly and a little shameless now, but it felt imperative at the time," Jeanie said. "Everyone who could get there, did."

*A showdown*, I marveled. I hadn't even known what was happening or that Flint was there until I asked Mary what was going on. I almost couldn't blame folks for not wanting to miss that.

I removed my phone from my pocket and searched for

the village website, then looked for a place to download the text notification app. "I'm getting on the notice list."

"It's very helpful," Jeanie said. "I don't have to remember what's going on anymore. I just wait for the texts and go where the fun is." She cringed. "Not that last night was fun. Usually I'm notified about flash sales and two-for-one events."

My phone searched uselessly for Wi-Fi, not finding a strong enough cell signal to download the app. I shoved the device back into my pocket. I'd have to try again later. "Have you ever sent a notice?" I asked. "Sally at Corner Cup mentioned using them for marketing. Is there a record of who creates each post?"

Wilhelmina looked around, losing interest in the conversation. "You can probably reach out to tech support and ask. Go from there."

"Did you know Mr. Flint well?" I asked, hoping to draw her back in. She'd called him Frank, so she must've known him better than I had. Or maybe the first-name basis was due to their age differences. She seemed old enough to be his mother. "Or maybe you know his wife?"

Wilhelmina raised penciled-on eyebrows. "The Flints are separated."

"Do you know what happened?" I asked.

She frowned at my blatant rudeness. "I'm afraid that's their personal business and none of mine. I try not to get involved."

"Of course," I said. "Sorry. I didn't mean to pry."

Jeanie glanced conspiratorially in my direction. "Tina owns Pop Off. That's the new gourmet popcorn store on Longwood and Main. You can find her there during business hours most days if you want to speak with her."

"Thanks." I knew the area, but it was a long bike ride, practically on the other side of town.

Cromwell had a small population but covered an enormous amount of land.

I needed to talk to Mrs. Flint, but I'd have to do it on a day I could catch a ride in the community truck.

"Do either of you know Dirk Yoder?" I asked, recalling the name of Flint's predecessor on Local Yum. "He was the original reviewer of Cromwell restaurants and cafés, and I'm not sure why he didn't continue the work."

The women exchanged curious looks.

"No," Jeanie said. "I've never met him, but he rents the old radio station as an apartment. I remember that because everyone hoped we'd get a new station. It was disappointing when the owner turned it into housing."

Wilhelmina shook her head. "I don't know him, but it would be nice to have a radio station again."

"I'll stop by there and see if I can catch him," I said. "For the record," I told Wilhelmina. "I didn't hurt Mr. Flint, and I don't know who sent that text blast, directing folks to my souffle stand, but I'm going to find out. If you write about me or Souffle the Day again, I hope you'll print that. My foods aren't poisoned, and I'm not a murderer. I plan to prove it."

She nodded and smiled awkwardly then excused herself.

Jeanie tipped her head toward the shop at our sides, inviting me into The Pretty Pantry.

I followed.

"I think you make her nervous," she said.

"Because she thinks I'm a murderer?"

Jeanie laughed. "Because you are Louisa Eggers, daughter of Victoria and Preston Eggers, heir to the Laurelwood estate and grounds. I'm pretty sure your grandmama bullied her in elementary school, and you shook everyone's world when you captured that killer not long ago."

"Grandmama was a handful," I said, smiling as we moved inside.

"And it sounds like you're on the case again," Jeanie added, steering the conversation back to my previous amateur investigation.

I sighed. "Last time I tried to find a killer, I had help. This time, the stakes feel higher, and I'm on my own." I briefly considered calling my friend, Bonnie, who lived in the next town. She'd helped me decorate Souffle the Day, and solve my ex-boyfriend's murder not long ago. But I hated to bother her. Bonnie dated the sheriff, and he didn't like it when she got involved in these things. I decided to wait a while longer before reaching out, but knowing I had the option was a comfort.

She led me to the counter and rested her elbows near a display of brightly colored organizers. "Speaking of your family," she said. "Your mama was in here earlier, and she's fit to be tied."

"About me?" I asked, my voice squeaking on the final word.

"No." Jeanie shook her head. "She thinks someone's stealing from her. At first she suspected it was your father, sneaking in while she was away and helping himself to things. Now she's questioning the staff."

"That's terrible."

Mama hadn't said a word about such things to me.

Jeanie nodded. "I know, and I couldn't believe she was telling me of all people, but I guess she remembers me from when my daddy's lumber company helped with that barn building project when we were young, and she trusts me. Or maybe she just didn't have anyone else to tell, but it was like the flood gates opened and she laid it all bare."

I cringed, hating that I hadn't been around for Mama when she needed an ear. "She wants me to come home," I said, confessing to Jeanie as Mama had.

"Of course she does. You're her only daughter, and she

loves you. She misses you. I already dread the day my daughter grows up and moves out. I'll be heartbroken."

I thought of Jeanie's baby, who was probably a toddler now, and wondered if I would have babies one day. If I did, would Mama be in their lives?

I hoped so.

"I don't think she expected you to stay in Meadowbrook when you moved."

"I know," I said, certain it was time I visited Mama and ended the long-running tension between us. I wasn't a kid anymore, and there wasn't any reason to hide. I'd set my path in life, and I was proud of it. Just like I was proud of the woman who'd made me who I was.

I'd have to stop by Laurelwood soon and tell her how much I loved and appreciated her.

The shop door opened and a pair of women came inside to ask Jeanie for help with their cluttered pantries.

I said my goodbyes and headed back into the day, Thelma's crate in my hands.

"We're going to have to visit your grandmama," I told her. "Not today, but soon."

*Bawk-aw!*

"I know. Let's get some water and visit the park to stretch your wings before we head home."

*Bawk-ah!*

"Oh!" I said, stopping in my tracks beside the bike rack.

Both tires on my bicycle were flat, and the gooseflesh racing over my arms suggested it hadn't been an accident.

## CHAPTER EIGHT

eadowbrook's community pickup came into view as I scanned the area for signs of someone upset enough to flatten my tires. I couldn't imagine who would attack my bike. Or why? Unless a townie had heard I killed a man last night and wanted to lash out a little.

Eli stood across the street at the end of the block, speaking with the county sheriff, Mason Wright. Mason's filthy white Jeep was parked behind the truck along the curb. Both men were catastrophically gorgeous and normally when they shared the same space, I found it hard to breathe. But at the moment, I was just relieved.

I wouldn't have to manage a bike with two flats and Thelma's carrier on my own.

"See that, Thelma?" I asked, pointing her crate toward the men. "Silver linings are everywhere."

*Bawk-ah!* ·

"I know," I said, turning her away. "It's too much hotness. We shouldn't look directly at them when they're together like that. But we could really use some help."

*Bawk-ah!*

I checked both ways before jaywalking toward them. "What do you think they're talking about?"

Thelma clucked out a lengthy guess while I admired their casual confidence and easy smiles.

Sheriff Mason Wright lived in Cromwell, but mainly worked in the neighboring village of Bliss, Cromwell's long-time rival, since Cromwell has its own small police department. He was handsome to a fault and madly in love with my friend Bonnie Balfour, a woman who ran a second-chance shop at the square in their town. She had a beloved cat named Clyde, so folks got a kick out of us together. Bonnie and Clyde with Thelma and Louisa. We got a kick out of it too. But Sheriff Wright wasn't a fan of civilians launching private investigations, which Bonnie tended to do, and I couldn't help wondering if Eli was tattling on me as I approached.

"Hello," I called, beetling across the road before a giant lumber truck reached our block.

Sheriff Wright frowned at the pet carrier in my grip, then lifted his hand in greeting. "Louisa, Thelma. I'm on my way back to Bliss. Sorry about what's going on here. Call if you need anything."

He shot Eli a pointed look, then turned and darted away before I could ask him anything important. Like what he knew about the Flint investigation. And why he always seemed to run away when I came around.

Eli looked from me to the carrier, then reached for the bedazzled pink crate. "May I?"

I cheerfully passed Thelma to him. My arms were tired, though I'd never admit it. "I didn't realize you and the sheriff were friends."

"We are," he said.

I waited for him to elaborate.

He watched me, his steady hazel gaze roaming my

features and heating my cheeks. "What are you two up to?"

I commanded myself not to rub the gooseflesh climbing my arms. "Looking for some wedding inspiration." Though we hadn't gotten to that part of our outing before some troublemaker cut the trip short. "Any chance Thelma and I can bum a ride home? My bike has a flat."

"Sure. Where'd you leave it? I'll toss it in the back and get the tire pumped up for you."

"Across the street." I pointed in the general direction. "We can walk. No sense in moving the truck yet."

"All right." Eli took my hand in his, and we jogged across the road.

The electricity coursing between our palms stretched up my arm and through my chest.

When he released me, I gasped. In relief and in regret.

He opened and closed his hand a few times, examining his fingers before raising his gaze to mine.

I looked away. "Here it is," I said, motioning to my hobbled bike.

"They're both flat," Eli said. "How'd that happen?"

I nudged one tire with the toe of my shoe. "They were like this when I came out of The Pretty Pantry."

Eli passed Thelma back to me, then crouched for a closer look at the damage. He gripped and prodded each tire until a puncture became evident in each.

My mouth opened, and a small strangled noise escaped.

Eli stretched to his full height and pulled the cell phone from his pocket. "I think it's time we call Officer Anthony."


At home, he stuck around for a bit, helping me feed the hens and clean Jack's and Jill's stalls. He seemed to be lingering, but I didn't have it in me to ask why. I feared the question would prompt his departure, and I liked having him near.

"So the wedding's on?" he asked, feeding Jack a carrot from the garden.

"I think so," I said, looking to Jill for a definitive response.

She brayed and bobbed her head in a way that seemed to answer affirmatively

I laughed. "Yep. There's going to be a wedding."

Eli patted Jack's side. "Congratulations."

"I made some lists of things to buy while I was in town, but ordering online is probably better. I'm going to send a packet around Meadowbrook too, listing everything I'd like to borrow for the day. I can make my own invitations and deliver them."

"What will you need to borrow? Maybe I have something you can use."

"Well…" I lifted a hand to tick off my fingers. "I'll need a whole lot of chairs to line up for the service. Then, I can move those to the tables for the reception dinner." I bit my lip. "I should probably borrow a few more tables too."

"Or you can collect blankets and serve the reception meal picnic-style," he suggested.

My heart kicked at the word picnic on Eli's tongue, and the year-long fantasy of sharing a picnic with him under a tree rushed to mind.

"Do you like picnics?" he asked.

I pressed my lips together and nodded. "A lot."

He smiled, and a wave of tension wound between us.

I dragged my gaze to the pasture outside the souffle stand. "I'll cook, but I'll ask for volunteers to bring side dishes and desserts."

Eli rubbed his stubbled cheek. "You've given this a lot of thought, and it all sounds good."

I shrugged. "It's a miniature donkey wedding. How can it not be perfect?"

He laughed. "All right. What will they wear?"

"Top hat for Jack. Lace veil for Jill. I can get both at a thrift shop, then make alterations as needed. Once I install the fence around their barn, I can wrap it in twinkle lights and tulle. Maybe put a sign outside their window."

"Do you have the fence?" he asked, scanning the yard.

"I bought everything I needed this spring. I also bought some items for enrichment."

His smile reached his eyes when he looked at me. "You've got a lucky animal family here."

"I think I'm the lucky one."

Thelma hustled past, clucking and chasing her flock.

"I have a good life here," I said. One worth fighting for.

We spent the rest of the afternoon together, chatting and laughing together, and occasionally with neighbors when they stopped by to check in, or walked past with their dogs. Somehow the noise of my investigation and the pressing fears that came with it, faded into the background, and I'd simply enjoyed the day.

Eli tugged a pair of work gloves from his back pocket and stretched them over his hands. "Feel like a fire tonight?" he asked, approaching a stack of firewood I'd requested he deliver weeks ago. "It doesn't look as if you've used any of the load I brought."

I looked around, stunned to see the sun would set soon and thankful for the dimming light. He must know by now. I'd only requested the delivery as an excuse for Eli to come over.

"We could put some of this to use, if you're up to it," he said.

"I'd like that. Thank you."

Eli selected a few pieces from the pile, then carried them to my stone firepit.

"I'll put away the flock."

I moved toward the cluster of hens, pushing them into

the pen outside their elaborate chicken coop, pondering where the day had gone. And why I wasn't any closer to understanding what had truly happened to Mr. Flint.

Or who'd flattened my tires.

Eli was crouched before the firepit upon my return. He'd arranged several logs and stoked a flame to life while I'd said goodnight to my feathered friends. He glanced over his shoulder, then motioned to a set of chairs he'd dragged close enough to feel the heat from the flames.

I took a seat and watched him for a long beat.

"Penny for your thoughts?" he asked, rubbing his palms together before taking the seat beside mine.

"Okay." I blew out a long breath. "I think whoever flattened my tires might've known I was looking into Flint's death."

Eli didn't look surprised. "You want to talk about it?"

"Actually, yeah. Are you sure you want to hear all this?"

He nodded, and I started talking.

I recapped my conversation with Jeanie and Wilhelmina as the sun sank into the horizon and twilight fell over our world.

He rubbed his hands on the arms of his chair when I finished. "I wish you weren't doing this again," he said, shifting forward to rest both forearms against his thighs. He clasped and unclasped his big hands between his knees. "It's dangerous and worrisome."

"I know." I locked my gaze with his when he turned to me, pleading with my stare and willing him to understand. "I love it here. Raising hens and baking souffles. Living in this idyllic community and not caring about anyone's heritage or legacy. Not thinking about the life I'll be forced to lead at some indeterminant point in the future."

"I get that," he said, sounding as if he really might. "Your name and family legacy come with a significant burden of responsibility. And you can avoid all that in here, at least for now."

"Exactly." I moved my attention to the fire. "I know it's selfish, and a man is dead, but I feel as if I'm grieving what might've been. I wanted the souffle stand to be a success, and I wanted to show people I can do big things. I can be a debutante and a strong, independent business woman at the same time. The two aren't mutually exclusive. And I might look like I'm in high school, but I'm twenty-six. I have a dual degree in agriculture and history. I'm not a child or a silly heart. Souffle the Day would've been big—if it hadn't been struck down before it had a chance."

"It's not selfish to worry about your business and future. Flint died, and that was a tragedy, but you're still here, and your life is going on. Souffle the Day is important to you. Making your dreams happen on your terms is important to you. You shouldn't feel guilty about any of that."

I nodded, speechless and touched with emotion. It'd been a long time since I felt as if anyone understood me, and I wasn't sure how to respond. A traitorous tear rolled over my cheek, and I laughed softly. "Sorry. Crying probably isn't the best way to prove how strong I am."

"Hey now. Tears don't show weakness. They show humanity, and you're going through a lot. I'd worry if you weren't upset. And I know you've done just fine on your own all this time. You're not weak or stupid. And trust me, Louisa. I can see you aren't a child."

I bit my lip, suddenly shy. "Thank you."

His lips twisted into a mischievous smile. "If you ever need reminding, let me know."

I sat back in my chair and grinned shamelessly at the fire. "I don't think you've ever told me what brought you to Meadowbrook. You know I'm biding my time before I have to take over the Laurelwood empire. What about you?"

"There's not much to know about me."

And I knew. There was something in his tone and posture. Someone had broken his trust, and the betrayal had cost him. I was pushing him, and it was too soon.

"Never mind," I said. "You don't have to answer that. It was too personal, and I understand. We can just enjoy the fire."

Eli looked my way once more. "I came here looking for peace."

"Did you find it?"

"Aye," he said, and the firelight danced in his eyes.

A thrill rolled through me as I imagined his affirmative response might have something to do with me.

"You know," he said. "Whatever is happening between you and your mom, you should try to fix it. A family who loves you is everything. It's a gift many would give anything to have, and you should foster that, if you want to keep it."

"I know. I've been thinking about that a lot lately. But family isn't always blood. Sometimes we choose our families. Sometimes they choose us."

"You want to be my family?" he asked. His cocked brow and teasing tone left me unsure of how to answer.

I rolled my head against the back of my chair and gazed at the stars. "Maybe. Probably not any kind of blood relation."

He laughed. "I should hope not."

Stars began to appear through the twilight, in the darkest pieces of sky, unhindered by lights and obstructions.

Heat from the fire warmed my cheeks and hands. "I didn't realize you and the sheriff were friends."

He grunted in response.

It wasn't an answer, and I suspected the men shared a secret. One Eli didn't want to share.

I understood. Sometimes if felt as if secrets were my life. I certainly kept more than my share of facts to myself. Like the fact I owned most of Meadowbrook after buying a mass amount of acreage at a steep discount when one of the founders needed to sell. The community truck was legally mine now too.

And I had every intention of seeing my amateur investigation through, regardless of what Eli or anyone else thought about it. The police were focused on what happened to Mr. Flint, but I needed to do whatever it took to save my business, my reputation and my dream. I'd gotten to the bottom of something similar before, and I was sure I could do it again.

Tonight I would enjoy the quiet moments with Eli, but tomorrow I would call Dirk Yoder, the original Local Yum columnist and find out how Mr. Flint had come to take his job.

And I would have a talk with the estranged Mrs. Flint as well.

# CHAPTER NINE

*I* didn't sleep well again, haunted by memories of my bike's flat tires.

Eli had delivered a replacement, but the overall message was received loud and clear. Someone wanted me to know they were watching me. Maybe it was a disgruntled townie. Or someone suspicious about my apparent involvement in Mr. Flint's death. But my gut said I wasn't that lucky.

My gut said two stabbed tires were a warning. How many people had overheard me speaking to Wilhelmina and Jeanie on the sidewalk before I went inside the shop? I suspected someone hadn't liked what they'd heard.

It took two pots of tea to prepare me for another trip into town after morning chores, and about an hour to convince myself I wasn't in any shape to pilot a bike.

Blessedly, the community pickup was available.

"Thanks for agreeing to drive me," I told Eli as he navigated the winding roads into town. He'd planned to deliver firewood in town today, so it only made sense for us to carpool.

"It's no problem. How's Thelma doing?"

"Okay," I said, slipping one finger through the barred

door of her crate to pet her feathery head. "She can be a nervous rider."

Thelma clucked a steady stream of complaints from her carrier secured between us as we motored along. She much preferred to travel by bicycle.

I suspected she didn't like the hum of the engine, the wind whipping through our open windows, or her inability to see what was going on outside the cab.

"Shh," I cooed. "Truck rides aren't so bad."

Eli cast a sidelong look in my direction. "Where are you going again?"

"Pop Off. It's on the corner of Longwood and Main."

"Isn't that a popcorn shop?"

I smiled sweetly but kept my eyes on the passing scenery outside my window. "That's the one."

Eli completed his deliveries in under an hour, then pointed the truck toward my destination. "Have you put together the list of items you need to borrow for Jack and Jill's wedding?" he asked. "If not, we could work on that when we get back to Meadowbrook. Maybe even take the list door to door."

"Sounds good. I'd like that."

My phone rang, and I pulled it from my crossbody bag for a look.

Mama's name and number centered the screen. I swiped the call away and waited to see if she called back.

"Is that your mother?" Eli asked, angling his chin toward the phone in my hand.

I frowned. "How did you know?"

"Because you're just staring at it, and you're not answering."

I sighed in relief when the phone remained silent.

"She'll keep calling," he said. "Better to talk to her and get it over with."

I turned my face to the open window and stretched an arm outside. Wind beat against my palm as I opened and closed my fist.

Eli made it sound simple, but there wasn't a scenario where talking to Mama would ever end. Not until one of us died. Even then, she'd probably haunt me. I imagined puttering around the empty halls and quiet grounds of Laurelwood, talking to Mama as I wandered, alone and lonely.

I'd be the one who didn't get a response then.

We slowed at a stop light, and Eli set his hand on Thelma's crate. "Are you crying?"

"No." I blinked the stinging emotion from my eyes. Eli and Thelma were in a truck, but clearly I was on an emotional roller coaster. "I'm fine."

Eli grunted.

"What?" I asked.

He looked at me, eyebrows raised. "Nothing."

The light changed, and we rolled ahead, silent and tense in a new, unpleasant way. I'd thought Eli and I had broken through some of the barriers of a new friendship last night when we'd talked by the fire, but in hindsight, we'd mostly talked about Meadowbrook. We both enjoyed the people, the peacefulness and our lives there. We didn't talk much about our lives or who we were before moving there. And we hadn't discussed the people we aspired to be.

"We really don't know one another, do we?" I asked.

Eli's lips formed a lazy half smile. "No, but I'd like to change that. If you're up for it."

"I am, but why does it sound as if you've issued a challenge?"

"Think of it as an invitation."

My cheeks heated immediately, and my thoughts went south.

"Would you be offended if I told you how much I like it when you blush?" he asked.

I groaned.

"I'm serious. Your blush makes it easy to know when you're happy or mad. Sometimes when you're embarrassed. I only wish I knew what it meant each time."

"With you around, it's usually the latter," I said, shaking my head at the unfortunate truth. It was a bigger confession than he'd likely realize.

Eli pulled his gaze from the road long enough to make me nervous. "Why would you ever be embarrassed around me?"

I stared straight ahead, hoping he would too. Thankfully we seemed to be the only vehicle on the road.

"You're one of my favorite people," he said.

I peeked at him, and heat rose over me again. "I am?"

"Aye." He nodded. "You and my wee sister, Ella." He smiled, and the expression lit his whole face.

I wanted to meet Ella immediately. "I didn't know you had a sister."

"One. And she is my sun. She's at university now, in Ireland."

"Is that where you went to school?"

"No. I attended college in the states."

My mood improved sharply. I didn't care if Eli had gone to college, but I liked that we had something in common, outside of Meadowbrook. We'd both pursued higher education.

He maneuvered the truck against the curb outside a small log cabin a moment later. The words Pop Off were painted on a carved wooden sign on the front lawn.

"Do you mind waiting here with Thelma?" I asked, gripping my door handle with nervous fingers. I'd have to ask him what he'd studied in school later. After I spoke with Mrs. Flint. "I won't be long."

Eli settled the engine and lifted his chin in agreement.

I climbed out and hurried over the cobblestone walkway to the small front porch, then let myself inside.

The large open showroom had big popcorn pieces painted on the wide-planked wooden floorboards and sporadically on the walls. A service counter at the back of the room boasted floor-to-ceiling shelving, each level filled with clear containers of the treat. Every plastic barrel had a different color combination and flavor label.

I was the only shopper.

"Hello!" A woman called looking up from her position at the counter. "Welcome to Pop Off!" She dabbed a tissue to the corner of one eye. Her face was puffy and red. She wore black from head to toe.

"Mrs. Flint?" I asked, approaching with caution. "I'm Louisa Eggers."

She dropped the expression of faux cheeriness. "You."

I lifted my hand in a small wave. "Hi."

"What do you want?"

I took a tentative step forward. I wasn't sure what I'd expected from her, but the possibility of thinly veiled anger hadn't crossed my mind.

She appeared to be my mother's age, without any of Mama's ageless grace. This woman was tall and lean, with a sporty black pixie cut and sharp brown eyes. She was beautiful in an edgy dramatic way, with ice pick heels and a designer body suit that vanished into the waist of her puffy legged slacks.

The overall look didn't fit our little hamlet, and I wondered if she bucked the norm intentionally or had been transplanted here and not yet adapted.

"You killed my husband. How dare you come here!"

I looked over my shoulder, afraid someone might've heard, but we were still alone.

I wasn't sure if that made me feel better or worse.

"No, ma'am," I said. "I didn't kill Mr. Flint. I heard he had a heart attack or an allergic reaction to something. I really don't know what happened. That's why I'm here."

She pulled her chin back, mouth agape. "What do you mean?"

The door opened and a pair of women came inside, perusing the store displays near the window.

I moved closer to Tina and lowered my voice before speaking again. "I hate what happened, and I'm trying to find answers. If your husband's death was truly a fluke, a bee sting or whatever, that's unthinkably awful. But if his death was something more, I want to know."

Mrs. Flint blinked puffy eyes and worked her jaw. Her gaze flipped to her customers, then back to me. "What do you mean, something more?"

I pressed my lips together and waited.

"The police are already looking into this," she said.

"I know, and I'm not trying to interfere. I'm just trying to make sense of something completely senseless."

"It was senseless," she said, swiping away a renegade tear.

"Was your husband at odds with anyone lately?" I asked softly. "Had he been acting strangely? Preoccupied or upset about something?"

Her eyes jerked back to mine, but she didn't speak.

"Was there someone else involved in your separation?" I asked.

"What?"

I wet my lips and forced myself to press on. "Is it possible that person wanted him out of the picture?"

Rage contorted her expression, and I leaned back.

Had I accused her of being an adulteress? And her hypothetical lover of being homicidal? Yes. Had I gone too far? Also yes.

I imagined apologizing and walking back out the door before I made everything worse.

But where would that leave me? My souffle stand? My reputation? My dream?

I bit my lip and waited for her response.

"I didn't have a lover," she whispered. "If that's what you're implying. I left my husband because I'd become the other woman, thanks to that stupid town website."

Her shoulders squared, and she set her jaw. "I was silly to agree to his proposal so quickly, without realizing he was already married to his job. Once the honeymoon phase passed, I became the interloper. Or at least that was what I'd thought. Until he started spending all that time with you."

"Me?" I yipped.

The shop door opened once more, letting three more customers inside.

She nodded slowly, her hooded gaze growing painfully pointed. "Yes. You," she seethed. "In that bizzarro storybook forest of yours. He claimed fascination with the concept and people, but it didn't take me long to realize when he said people, he meant you." Her lips curled in distaste. "With your golden curls and big doe eyes. He claimed to love the way I stood out in a town of dowdy farm girls and aging southern belles. Men are so fickle."

I squirmed, wholly aware of the silence around us, despite five shoppers. "Mr. Flint was researching for a story on Meadowbrook and my souffle stand. There wasn't anything like what you're suggesting going on. I was shocked when he posted a review of the place. He told me the article would be an interest piece. I don't know why he lied."

I realized for the first time as I spoke that I was hurt by the review and his deception. And I'd never be able to tell him how I felt or understand why he'd done it. His unfair words were also unkind, unprovoked and... mean. His post had the power to sway townies' ideas about my entire community and way of life.

She pushed her wedding ring in circles with her thumb, eyes distant and newly unfocused. "He was supposed to realize how much he loved me and come running back. Now everything is unresolved, and I'll never know why he didn't think I was enough. Because I am enough," she growled. "And he's dead. And I can't even tell him how angry I am!"

I stepped back.

Another shopper came inside, stopped to take in the scene, then left.

The remaining customers seemed caught between fascination and fear, unsure if they should bolt or grab some popcorn for the showdown.

I mentally calculated the paces to the door and how fast I could make the trek if she reached for me.

"Do you know what it's like to lose someone?" she asked, thin brows furrowed and voice hard. "How absolutely infuriating it is when it happens too soon and there's no warning and it's not fair at all that they're gone? And you were arguing so the last thing you said to them was probably something heinous, but you can't take it back, and now you have to live with it forever. But they don't, because they left you!"

I swallowed hard and fished a handkerchief from my purse, then offered it to her.

She rolled her eyes and walked around to the business side of her counter, then reached underneath. She set a bright-pink purse between us and pulled out a travel pack of tissues.

I put the hanky back in my pocket, struggling to recall what it was about the purse that held my attention. "I'm sorry," I said, watching helplessly as she dried her eyes and attempted to calm down. "I didn't come here to upset you."

I reinforced the mental note to call my mother. She made me crazy, and we had our share of disagreements, but at least she was still around to argue with.

"Mrs. Flint," I said, testing my voice again. "Before he died, your husband asked me what was in the quiche. Do you have any idea why would he ask that? Did he have some kind of allergy?"

"Soy," she said, deflating against the counter for support. "The police already told me the coroner suspected anaphylaxis. I told them he can't eat soy. He has an EpiPen but never remembers to take it anywhere. He's meticulous about his diet. Was," she corrected, then choked on whatever she'd planned to say next.

"I'm sorry," I said softly, wishing there were more and better words. "I don't use soy," I added, immeasurably relieved by that. "I bake with milk, cream and butter from the neighbor's cows."

Her gaze shifted away, then back. I would've given anything to read her thoughts.

"Do you know Dirk Yoder?" I asked, sensing my time and her patience for me was reaching an end. "He's the man who started the Local Yum column."

She dropped her tissue in a waste can behind her. "Dirk Yoder is a self-important brat and a pouty puss. He started something he didn't have time to manage, then got angry when someone who could make it their priority stepped in."

"So, he and Mr. Flint didn't get along?"

"No."

"Does the columnist position pay?" I asked, wrinkling my nose for being rude once more. No one, aside from my mother, wanted to talk about money.

"Absolutely. The town paid Dirk to set up the website as a means of encouraging travelers to give us a try. The idea was to showcase what we have to offer here. Once that was finished, and the initial articles were up, the city needed someone to continue providing new content and website management. Dirk didn't have time for all that. Frank did."

My mouth opened, then closed. "So, Mr. Flint took Dirk Yoder's job? After he'd set up the site and populated it with articles?"

She shrugged. "My husband was the better writer, and he had the time and experience necessary to do the job well." She tucked the tissue pack into her purse with a look of superiority. "The village chose him for a reason."

Mr. Flint was a decent writer. Normally. But not in the brief review he'd posted about Souffle the Day. I put that and the Dirk Yoder questions aside as her bright-pink purse snagged my attention once more. "Is that an Sophia Cardiff?" I asked. Sophia Cardiff was a local leatherworker and handbag designer who charged an arm and a leg for custom, one-of-a-kind creations. My mother adored her. And I'd recognize her work anywhere.

I'd seen it at Souffle the Day on the afternoon Mr. Flint died.

Another round of shoppers entered and decided to stay.

"Yes," she said, suspicious once more. "Why?"

I tried to appear relaxed, though my cheeks burned hotter than the sun. I'd been warned all my life never to make a spectacle of myself, but here I was, talking to a possible killer and accumulating an audience.

Why in the world hadn't she mentioned she was present when her husband died? Did the police know?

"I saw it the other day. At my souffle stand."

"No. You didn't." She moved the purse out of sight, putting it behind service counter without another word. "I think we're done here."

I nodded my goodbye, in complete agreement, then scuttled out the door.

Relief washed over me at the sight of Eli's face. He smiled and spoke to someone inside the truck, presumably Thelma, unless he'd made a phone call. In which case, I wished I knew who'd made him smile that way.

"I'm back," I said, opening the door and flopping onto the passenger seat.

"Welcome." Eli started the engine. No cell phone in sight.

I checked on Thelma then buckled up.

Outside the window, pedestrians watched with curiosity. I recognized several from inside the shop.

Hadn't they ever seen a woman confront a scary but grieving widow, then run away from a popcorn shop before?

"All right," I said. "Let's go."

Eli dragged his gaze over the cluster of shoppers staring at us from the cobblestone path. "Friends of yours?"

"Yep." I lifted a hand to wave. "Bye y'all," I said brightly. "Nice seeing you again!"

My chauffeur shifted into gear and carried us away.

CHAPTER TEN

*E*li parked in my driveway an hour later, and I set Thelma free in the yard.

"Thanks for driving me into town. And for taking us to the park so Thelma could stretch a little before coming home. It means a lot."

Eli leaned against the pickup's hood. "It's no problem."

He watched the other hens race to greet Thelma, chuckling when they swept her into their cloud of feathers and ushered her away.

"I've got sweet tea inside," I said. "If you don't have other plans, I can pour us some."

He pushed away from the truck as I noticed a package on my porch.

I tucked the small box against my side as I unlocked my door to let us in.

"Expecting a delivery?" he asked.

"Maybe." I set the box on the kitchen counter to pour two glasses of sweet tea. My nerves were rattled after my chat with Tina Flint, and I needed a moment to think.

The package was addressed to me at the souffle stand. I supposed it might be another item I'd ordered for the décor.

I ferried two full glasses of iced tea to the table and gave the innocuous box a closer inspection. "I found a thrift shop in Atlanta who sends me vintage kitchen supplies for the café's displays."

He turned the package to face me. "Do they commonly omit a return address?"

I chugged my tea, feeling the icy fingers of dread curl around my core.

The box wasn't in great shape. The tape across its top was crooked and warped. The address label was printed not handwritten. "Let's just open it and solve the mystery," I teased, still hoping for an antique flower sifter or canister.

The tape peeled off easily, the sticky sound tightening my muscles. The weight was right for any number of kitchen gadgets, and something hard had knocked around inside the box.

I parted the cardboard flaps, and a set of black binoculars came into view. Both lenses were cracked.

Eli liberated the item and frowned. "You ordered this?" he asked, turning the strange item over in his hands.

I shook my head, then reached for the packing slip at the bottom of the empty box. "Definitely not."

The single sheet of white paper had been folded in half beneath the binoculars. I stilled as four words came into view.

Stop Looking For Trouble

Eli swore.

My phone began to ring before my mind could catch up with my racing heart. I slid one thumb across the screen to ignore my mother's call.

"You'd better sit down," Eli said, removing the note from my trembling hand. "Sip your tea and breathe."

He set the paper and binoculars on my table and used his phone to take photos of both.

I rubbed the slow throb in my temples.

"Here." Eli passed me the bottle of ibuprofen from my countertop, where I kept a little first aid kit.

I accepted absently.

"Drink." He nudged the tea closer.

I obeyed, despite my strange out-of-body experience. "This is a threat."

Eli leaned against my island, gaze fixed on the broken binoculars and note. "Yes."

"And two flat bike tires," I said, forcing myself to accept the thing I'd done my best not to think about.

"Seems that way. Though this is much more concerning. This isn't someone who took an opportunity to aggravate you. This person made a plan, wrote a note, then had it delivered or came to your door."

"Escalation." That wasn't good. Unless I'd upset two different people. One who'd flattened my tires and another who'd sent this warning. It seemed unlikely I'd have more than one stalker in the same little time frame.

My phone dinged with the notification of a new voicemail. Mama had left a message.

I washed down two pills with the remainder of tea in my glass.

Eli pushed his untouched drink in front of me.

I drank half before stopping to catch my breath.

"Better?"

I glanced at the binoculars and note. "Not really. I should call the police, right?"

"You have to. This is a direct threat."

"Maybe we should first find out if anyone saw the

package being delivered," I suggested. Mostly because getting law enforcement involved meant this was real, and I was likely being threatened by a killer again. The police would undoubtedly want to know why. Then, they'd be upset I'd been asking questions about Mr. Flint's death, and their attention would become refocused on me instead of looking for the real killer.

"Putting off the inevitable won't change anything," Eli said.

My eyes widened, and I feared he was reading my mind.

"I see those mental wheels turning. Don't overthink. Just rip off the bandage and make the call."

"Rushing won't help either. I just want to get my head around this first."

"Around the delivery or Mr. Flint's murder?"

I averted my gaze. "Both."

The air between us thickened. "Louisa," he said, half-pleading, half-irate. "You need to leave this murder alone. The time could come when this criminal stops sending neatly packaged threats and starts trying to hurt you."

I flinched. "Maybe, but people think I poisoned a man." I caught Eli's eyes again and waited for the words to sink in. "Even if a few people are willing to give me the benefit of the doubt, they'll never eat at Souffle the Day again, because even if I'm not a murderer, he died eating my food."

Eli's expression softened, and he dropped into a squat before me. "I understand what you're saying, but we don't know anything about Frank Flint or who might've had it in for him. There are a lot of bad people in the world. We both came here to avoid them."

"What about my reputation and livelihood?" I asked, raising my brows in challenge. "The reputation of our community. At what point do I stop hiding and fight back?"

I wondered once more about the catalyst that had pushed

Eli to move to Meadowbrook. What had his life been like before?

"You don't trade your life for reputation or business," he said. "Reputations and incomes can be revived. You cannot."

I swallowed hard, and an ice cube of terror slid down my spine. If a killer had come to my door, one of my hens could've been injured, or worse, by this person who had no respect for life.

"You still aren't dialing," Eli said.

I straightened, meeting his worried gaze with mine. "Flint's wife had enough time to do this. We stopped for ice cream, and we walked at the park."

Memories of her barely tamped down temper rushed back to me. If Tina had killed her husband, she probably wasn't thrilled to know I was hunting answers instead of being a compliant scapegoat.

"Think about it," I said. "She could've left Pop Off when we did, then come straight here. She'd be long gone by now, because we made two more stops."

Eli furrowed his brows. "Flint's wife was at Pop Off?"

I pursed my lips. "She owns the shop."

He groaned and stretched to his full height, looking down at me as if he wanted to scream or rant. Instead, he ground his teeth and narrowed his eyes. "What did you say to her?"

"I asked about her husband. And I saw her purse outside Souffle the Day on the night he died, so I asked her about that too."

Eli scowled.

"She was his wife," I said. "I figured she'd know if he had any enemies. Or allergies. He does, by the way. Soy. I don't use soy, so I should be cleared by the police soon. I'll have to make sure Wilhelmina prints that. Oh, and get this," I added, picking up speed. "Mrs. Flint claims she wasn't here the night he died, which is a lie. That handbag designer only makes one-of-a-kind products. So, unless her purse was stolen, she was definitely here."

"How do you know the artist didn't make an exception or change their practices?"

I sighed. "My mother loves those bags. She owns a ton, and Sophia Cardiff is as rigid and set in her ways as Mama. Change is a four-letter word to people like them."

"Is it possible your mother killed Flint?" Eli asked.

I pulled my chin back and furrowed my brows. "No. That's ridiculous."

"Why? I'm not saying she did, but if she's the villain you make her out to be, it could be a great way to tank your life here and force you home."

"My mother is not a killer. And she'd never be caught dead carrying anything hot pink or adorned with yellow pompoms. Mrs. Flint was definitely here that night. I just don't know why she'd lie about it."

Eli lifted a palm in surrender.

I finished the second glass of tea, then stood. My blood pressure dropped a little and the world darkened before brightening once more.

Eli set his hand on my arm to steady me. "You okay?"

"Mm hmm." I started for my front door. "I'm going to see if anyone noticed the package being delivered. Then I'll call the police."

I made it as far as the porch before a familiar vehicle appeared at the bend in the road. "Here comes Murray," I said.

Murray was a botanist who grew a number of specialized plants and delivered them around town to property owners, nurseries and landscaping companies. His four-wheeler was hooked up to a flatbed trailer used for hauling small loads. Today it was covered in trees, bundled and wrapped as if for

Christmas, but more likely for a backyard rejuvenation project in town.

I'd been meaning to talk to him about the wedding. Now I had a second reason.

Eli followed me into the grass at the edge of my driveway, and I waved an arm overhead as Murray drew near.

The four-wheeler slowed, then stopped before us.

"Hey there, Ms. Louisa," he called. "Eli." Murray's round head was bald and sunburned. He'd moved to Meadowbrook after a heart attack and twenty years in banking. Like everyone else in town, he knew my mother, so I had to be careful what I said. "What's good in the neighborhood?"

"Everything's great here," I said. "How's your day?"

"Much better now," he said with a playful wink. "I'm on my last delivery."

"That's great." I smiled and Murray beamed back. "Speaking of deliveries, did you happen to see a package being delivered here on one of your trips in and out today?"

He glanced toward my front door. "I surely did," he said, stroking the length of his short gray-and-brown beard. "Jim was at your door when I came back from dropping off a mess of hydrangeas to the Baptist church on Pillar Street. Why? Wasn't it there when you got home?"

"Oh, it was there," Eli muttered, reminding me he was at my side.

Murray's gaze bounced from Eli to me. "Do you need something taken back to the UPS store for ya? I can drop it off on my way through town."

I shook my head. "No, that's all right."

"Jim delivered the package?" Eli asked.

"That's right."

Jim was our usual delivery person and had been delivering to Meadowbrook long before I'd arrived. He made same-day deliveries in Cromwell with his old box truck, and he accepted tips like any formal ride-share service. Expect he didn't care what he transported. If it fit in his truck, he'd haul it.

I forced my shoulders back and brightened my expression. "Thanks, Murray. I'll catch Jim when he comes through again tomorrow."

"All righty," he replied, smiling once again. "Anything else I can do for ya?"

"Any chance I could have a bunch of potted shrubs and flowers delivered for a backyard wedding?" I clasped my hands at my waist and brightened my smile. "Just for the day. Invitations haven't gone out, but you're invited, of course. The whole community will be."

Murray leaned back in his seat and released a hoot. "I knew it." I knew there was something going with y'all. I've been saying that for months! Congratulations." He extended a hand to Eli. "Couldn't have happened to a nicer fella. This one here is a keeper." He turned his eyes to me when Eli didn't take his hand. "He'll treat you right," he said, unfazed by Eli's rejection. "All your sunshine melted a little ice off this mountain, am I right?" He chuckled. "Count me in on whatever y'all need." He set his palms on the steering wheel before I could form a response. "Take care now!"

"It's for Jack and Jill," I called as Murray drove away. "It's not—"

I turned slowly to Eli, shock and embarrassment surely turning my face crimson.

The corner of his mouth turned up as he gazed down at me. "How long do you think it'll take for news of our nuptials to spread through town?"

I inhaled deeply and walked past him to my door. "I have to call the police."

Eli followed. He leaned against the archway in my living room while I collapsed onto a chair. "We might be able to catch Jim after he finishes his route tonight. Or plan to meet him at his office before he heads out tomorrow."

I paused to eyeball my flip-flopping friend. His words sounded more like a suggestion to dig in than to let this go. "Let's try to catch him tonight, after the cops come and take this." I pointed at the box, binoculars and note on my table.

I unlocked my phone and saw the voicemails I still needed to check. "Give me a minute to listen to Mama's message, then I'll call Officer Anthony."

I entered my access code and waited for the new voice message to play.

"Hello, Louisa," Mama said pleasantly, an unmistakable cord of tension tightening each word. "I heard about the commotion at your egg shop, and I wanted to see if there's anything I can do for you. Since I can't reach you, you'll have to come tomorrow for tea so we can discuss it and the other thing we spoke about over coffee." She disconnected without goodbye, and I knew she'd hold me to the tea.

"You look pale," Eli said.

I tipped forward and thunked my head against the table.

*a*s predicted, Officer Anthony wasn't happy when she arrived to collect the evidence and make a report. She told me to stop butting into her investigation and appraised me with unveiled suspicion, despite the threats made against me. She spoke to a few neighbors and Eli before leaving, and I'd breathed a heavy sigh of relief to see her go.

The whole encounter didn't make for a great night's sleep. My second terrible night in a row.

I dragged myself out of bed at sunrise, determined to stay off the police's radar moving forward and to take a nap after my chores.

Once the hens were fed, I scrambled two eggs with diced bell peppers and cheese, then carried the omelet onto my back patio, along with a cup of coffee. The sun was hot on my skin when I sat, and the coffee quickly warmed my belly.

Thelma and her entourage clucked and pecked around the little yard outside their hen house.

I watched their carefree exchanges and simple contentment, envying them that. I didn't have siblings, and my closest cousins lived in Louisiana, so my life had significantly more solitude than Thelma's. But I was thankful for her presence in mine.

Jack and Jill brayed and meandered, enjoying their morning, while I finished my breakfast.

Today seemed like a good day to start the pasture fence and enrichment playground. Maybe create the wedding invitations and a sign-up list for help with items I'd need to borrow.

My stomach tightened with the memory of Murray's awkward misunderstanding. I'd have to make things clear as I passed the sign-up sheet around. The donkeys were getting married. Not Eli and me.

I rubbed my forehead, refusing to think about that dream, especially how it would end. With sweet words and joined hands. A kiss that promised more.

I puffed my cheeks, tearing myself away from the fantasy. The kissing was a nice image. The marriage, not as much. Look at how that had worked out for my folks. Split up after more than twenty years.

Souffle the Day caught my attention in the distance, silent and empty. I frowned at the possibility I might never reopen, then forced the idea away. Mary handled the brooding. I was in charge of silver linings. And I needed one now more than ever.

I also needed to call my mother. If I didn't set a time for tea at her place soon, she could show up at mine, and a surprise visit from her would send me over the edge.

Thelma turned and headed in my direction as I dialed.

*Bawk-ah!*

"Good morning," I said. "This is going to be a stay-home-and-build-a-donkey-playground day. No snooping. No investigating. No poking proverbial bears."

She cocked her head and pointed one beady eye at me. *Bawk-ah!*

*Bawk-aw!*

*Bawk-aw!*

*Bawk-aw!*

I set my phone aside, watching as Thelma clucked and strutted at my feet, ranting about something I didn't understand.

"We aren't going anywhere. No bike rides. No parks and ice cream. I'm hiding out and minding my own business because there's a good chance a killer wants to murder me." I drew a finger across my throat like a saw.

She increased the strutting and screaming, as if she wanted me to get up and run.

The thought sent a shiver down my spine, and I pushed away from the patio table. I scanned the yard and field beyond. No signs of lurking lunatics. Still, I couldn't shake the foreboding that settled into my bones.

"I'm going to go inside for a bit," I told Thelma. "You're welcome to come, or I'll check on y'all again after I do a few things."

She flapped her wings and followed me inside.

I locked up behind us and went to check the front door lock too.

"I guess yesterday's package shook me more than I realized," I told her. I needed a moment to catch my breath. "At least the note at the bottom of the box warned me to stop looking for trouble. It could've said something much scarier like, I'm going to kill you. Instead, it was just a warning." My second chance to butt out.

I flipped the deadbolt on the front door as a police cruiser pulled into my driveway.

Thelma flapped onto the couch in front of my window and went bananas again.

Officer Anthony closed her car door and levered

sunglasses onto the top of her head. She squinted at my house, then headed for the porch.

I went to greet her, hoping she had good news. Thelma followed me outside.

*Maybe Mr. Flint was killed by a bee.*

*Or the police found and arrested the person who'd flattened my tires and threatened me.*

*Maybe my souffle stand was clear to reopen.*

"Ms. Eggers," Officer Anthony said, slowing as she approached. She passed a tri-folded set of papers to me.

"Good morning," I said. "What's this? Good news, I hope."

"I have a warrant to search the kitchen in your home and your souffle stand."

"What?" I glanced at the papers. The word Warrant stood at the top of the page. "Why?"

She moved toward me, forcing me to step aside or be barreled over. "Pardon me."

I followed her into my home, leaving Thelma to stare after us. My gaze bounced between the officer and the document in my grip. "I don't understand. Please explain what's happening."

Officer Anthony stopped at the threshold to my kitchen and raised a palm between us. "I'm going to have to ask you to wait here until I finish. Any interference can result in your arrest. I'll come for you when I finish, then we'll move on to the souffle stand."

I shook the crinkling pages. "Explain this."

She shoved her hands into a pair of blue plastic gloves, releasing each with a crack. "Coroner's report is in. Mr. Flint's death was caused by anaphylaxis as suspected. His stomach contents revealed the ingestion of a lethal amount of soy. Mr. Flint had a severe and known allergy to soy and would not have consumed this intentionally."

"He was poisoned," I said, unsure how I felt about the

confirmation.

The officer nodded. "Seems that way."

"With soy." An image from an old spy movie crossed my mind. The killer wore a large ring that unlatched. I imagined it playing out at Souffle the Day. The jeweled top swung away to reveal a small hollowed center filled with soy, which the killer covertly spilled into Mr. Flint's drink.

Then boom.

Man down.

"I'm not at liberty to discuss the details of an ongoing homicide investigation," Officer Anthony said. "Please wait here while I search your kitchen."

I stumbled back and knocked my calves into my sofa, so I took a seat.

I listened as the officer bumped and banged around in the next room, digging through my refrigerator and freezer, then sifting through my cupboards. "I don't have any soy," I said. "I only cook and bake with ingredients grown or produced in Meadowbrook. I use milk, cream and butter from the neighbors' cows." I'd told Mr. Flint that more than once during his time researching for the story he'd said he was writing. We'd discussed the farm-to-fork ingredients used in my recipes at length. He'd been pleased.

Until he wasn't. And the awful review popped up online.

"Uh huh," she said, not looking up as she spoke.

"Have you had any luck finding the person who sent me that note and those binoculars?" I asked.

"Not a top priority right now."

I tipped forward to rest my forearms on my thighs and wrung my hands. I wanted to curl into a ball and scream or march into the kitchen and ask if she really believed I might've hurt Mr. Flint. Over one bad review.

"The entire department is working around the clock on this murder case," Officer Anthony said, projecting her voice through my home. "The binoculars, box and note went to the lab for prints. It's the best we can do for now. You don't have any security cameras in this community, and no one I spoke with yesterday had any idea who would send that to you."

I huffed. "Flint's killer obviously sent it. Murray saw Jim deliver it. Are you even planning to talk to them?"

Eli and I had missed Jim at the end of his workday, but Eli volunteered to look for him today, and I'd easily agreed.

Officer Anthony fixed me with an impatient stare. "I've already spoken with Jim," she said. "He didn't remember where the package you received came from. He said he sees a lot of packages. Nothing about yours gave him pause. No reason for it to have stood out. And according to Jim his memory isn't what it used to be." She closed her eyes for a beat, and I suspected she might be rolling them behind her lids.

I huffed. The Jim lead was a bust, and I needed a break.

"And why are you looking in my house for his murder weapon?" I added. "Whoever killed Mr. Flint has threatened me."

Officer Anthony reappeared, empty-handed. "It's my job to follow the facts. That's what I'm doing. Besides, searching your property will serve as one more thing in your favor if I don't find anything. You can rest a little easier. No soy. No smoking gun." She lifted her hands, palms up. "Let's take a look inside the café."

I grabbed my keys and nodded. "Okay, but if I'm the killer, who sent me that threat?"

She frowned and shrugged. "I don't know how many people you've upset lately. Maybe you're in more than one person's business."

"Wow."

She shook her head, expression mildly apologetic. "Look. I'm not trying to be rude. I'm just saying, this isn't the first murder investigation where you've been an obstacle. It doesn't seem like a stretch to think you might get involved in other things you shouldn't. Maybe it's a personality flaw. Maybe you're naturally nosy. Or bored. I don't know. And that's not my job to decide. I'm just here to look for soy. And hopefully figure out how it got into Mr. Flint's meal that night."

I sighed. It was the longest speech I'd ever heard her give. And she was right. She didn't know me, and she was just trying to do her job.

My doorbell rang, and Mary walked inside before I could reach the knob.

"Why is there a police cruiser in your driveway?" she asked, eyes fixed on Officer Anthony.

The officer peeled off her gloves and tossed them in my trash. "The souffle stand," she said, brows tented in a *let's go, I don't have all day* prompt.

"Right." I turned to Mary. "She has a warrant to check my kitchen and the café for soy. Want to walk with us?"

Mary glowered. "Yes."

I led the way through my back door and across the sea of green grass.

My hens had fanned out over the lawn, exploring delight-edly, while Jack and Jill grazed near their barn.

I turned to Mary as we walked. "Did you only come over to ask about the cruiser, or did you need something?"

Her eyes widened a fraction before returning to their typically unimpressed expression. "I wanted to talk to you about a job opportunity."

I released a long breath, hating the fact I was partly the reason she had to look for other work, and my phone rang. I peeked at the number, then rejected the call. My mother was going to drive over and drag me to Laurelwood by my ear if I didn't answer soon or set up that tea time.

"Sorry," I said, when I caught Mary watching me stow the phone away. "I need to call Mama when Officer Anthony finishes here. She wants me to come for tea, and I've been avoiding it. I didn't mean to interrupt you." I stopped outside the café and unlocked the barn doors for the officer, swinging both open wide. "Let's talk while she looks inside." I tipped my head to the nearest picnic table.

Mary and I had a seat outside the open souffle stand while Officer Anthony explored my freezer, inspecting the vacant shelves and full ice bin.

I dragged my gaze to Mary, giving her my complete attention and an encouraging nod. "Tell me about your job opportunity."

Hopefully this conversation would be moot after Officer Anthony finished her work.

"It's at Laurelwood," Mary said.

I squinted. "Sorry, what?"

"Laurelwood. For your mom."

I struggled to maintain my fading smile. "I don't understand."

"Your mom offered me a full-time position as a character at the living museum for the rest of the season. She even said she would buy some of my eggs each week for her brunches."

My left eye twitched, and I pressed the pad of one finger against the convulsing skin. "Really."

"Yes. And all I had to do to secure the position was make sure you had tea with her, which it already sounds as if you plan to do. So, will you please make those plans as soon as possible?"

My head dropped forward, and I groaned. "You're going to work for my mother. At Laurelwood."

"As long as you have tea with her in the next few days, yes," Mary said. "Then everything is fixed, and it doesn't matter how long this pointless investigation into the souffle stand takes."

I raised my head to tell her, again, that I'd made plans to sell some of her eggs at The Weathervane but stopped when I heard Officer Anthony's footsteps return.

"Eggers," she said, my glass container of cream in one gloved hand. "This isn't cow's milk or cream."

I pushed onto my feet and moved in her direction as she bagged the bottle of liquid. The contents moved strangely inside the glass, without clinging to the sides the way they should.

"It's soy," she said. "I've got the opposite problem Mr. Flint had. I'm lactose intolerant, and I know soy."

"That's impossible," I said. "I don't use soy. No one raises it here, and I don't buy it. Let me see."

She snatched the bag back, scowling as if she might try to arrest me if I pressed the issue. "This is evidence now. Once the lab confirms its contents, you're going to have a lot of explaining to do. Starting with why you lied to a police officer."

CHAPTER TWELVE

*I* returned to my home alone. Bone-crushing gratitude carried me inside, and I thanked my lucky stars I hadn't been arrested immediately for a crime I didn't commit. The fact Mary went home without a scene, instead of imploding from rightful outrage, was another blessing.

I flopped onto the couch and called Mama to set a time for tea while I was still a free woman. Today seemed like the best option, all things considered. When I finished speaking with Mama, I took a chance and dialed the contact number I found on the Town Yum for Dirk Yoder. The moment Officer Anthony found soy in my café's fridge, I no longer had the luxury of letting the investigation take its course. I had to suck up my apprehension and get back in the game.

Dirk Yoder didn't answer, so I added him to my contact list and sent him a text.

An hour later, I examined myself in the mirror, dressed in something Mama had bought me when I still lived at Laurelwood. Thankfully I'd had the forethought to keep a few such clothing items on hand when I moved to Meadowbrook. My current wardrobe made Mama sneer.

I turned to examine my reflection from every angle. My body had changed in the years since a tailor had adjusted the pieces to my figure. The muted curves of a pampered young woman had become sharper and more distinct with age. Hard work on my property and countless miles walked and biked had shaved my round edges and tightened my core. Now, my merely adequate bosom appeared ample above a whittled waist, and my distinctly average backside had grown round from a thousand squats tending hens, pulling weeds and cleaning stables.

The cream blouse was loose across my chest, and my pencil skirt hung lower on narrowed hips than it ever had before. But at least the ensemble still fit.

I tried two more options, before settling on a knee-length sundress with narrow straps and a cinched empire waist. The pale-yellow color reminded me of the lemon trees outside my bedroom window at Laurelwood. I could almost smell the buds in bloom as I pulled the zipper up my side. Next I brushed my hair and twisted it into a pair of space buns to keep me cool, then grabbed my mini-backpack and donned my most comfortable sneakers.

Someone had borrowed the community pickup, and I wasn't ready to ride my bike again. The bicycle had felt dangerous since the tires were flattened. How would I know if someone had also loosened the wheels or damaged my steering? What if I was halfway down a mountain and something went catastrophically wrong?

I definitely needed to have it inspected for mechanical integrity.

The sound of a distant four-wheeler caught my ear, but it wouldn't do me any good. ATVs were great for hauling things through Meadowbrook; they weren't legal to drive on standard roads.

I pursed my lips and scanned the road in each direction, hoping I'd somehow missed the small white truck. Then I turned toward the Meadowbrook exit and started walking.

Another of my many secrets? I'd never learned to drive. Usually that wasn't a problem, because someone was around to drive me.

I pressed yellow-framed sunglasses over my eyes as I stepped into the sweltering heat of a bright summer day. I'd need to refill my water bottle before leaving Mama's place because it was sure to be empty when I arrived.

My phone dinged, and I read the display.

Dirk Yoder: I have time now if your available

I frowned. He'd used the wrong form of *you're*. Was poor grammar and spelling a new trend in website reviewers?

The phone dinged again before I could respond.

Dirk Yoder: I'll be home for about an hour. The old radio station.

The familiar zip of excitement danced in my chest as I typed out a response.

Me: On my way!

I picked up my pace, eager to have as much time as possible with Dirk Yoder and hoping he wouldn't mind speaking with me outside. Just in case he was a killer.

Anything I learned during our chat would give me material to busy my thoughts during tea. And reduce my urge to snap when Mama inevitably poked fun at my hair. My sneakers. My lifestyle. Hopefully the conversation with her wouldn't revolve around my duty to run the family estate. Or devolve into another push for me to marry soon and properly. Which was to say in accordance with her specific rules and guidelines. Not for love. Certainly not for passion.

According to Mama, I required a man of good breeding,

whose reputation wasn't of ill report. A man with money, who would do exactly what I said, when I said it, and thank me for giving the orders.

My very own robot with a trust fund. How could I resist?

My feet slowed to a crawl as I imagined the conversation.

*Come on*, I willed myself forward, entering the small downtown area's edge. Time was of the essence. I sent Mama a quick text to let her know I planned to make a stop on my way, then I focused my thoughts on Dirk Yoder.

I'd never met him, and from what I'd gathered, he was fairly new to Cromwell, so there was a chance he wouldn't recognize me. The message I'd left on his voicemail was intentionally vague. I'd waffled between being straight with my questions—and potentially provoking a murderer—or being coy. The former seemed the obvious choice. If he was the killer who'd been leaving me threats, then there wasn't much point in beating around the bush. On the other hand, if he was innocent, and I was just a lady with some questions, there wasn't any reason to fear he'd kill me later.

Being a straight shooter seemed the way to go.

My phone dinged, and I gave it another look.

The message was from Dirk Yoder.

Dirk Yoder: Are you still coming?

I lengthened my stride, fearful he might change his mind and leave before I arrived. I hit the crosswalk button at the street corner, urging the light to change so I could keep walking.

I responded to Mr. Yoder while I waited.

Me: Almost there!

The light turned green, and I hustled across the road and down the next block toward the old radio station, where he lived. Busier streets bled into semi-residential areas, where homes and home-based businesses loosely lined the land-scape. Small parks and trailheads for the county hike-and-bike path interspersed the buildings. A steepled church with a large accompanying cemetery stretched along the eastern valley.

By the time I reached Mr. Yoder's address, I was out of breath and sweaty in places he probably wouldn't notice and I didn't want to think about.

I knocked on the exterior storm door and waited.

There didn't seem to be a doorbell, but the large wooden door beyond the one I'd already tapped on had a brass lion's head knocker with a thick round ring in its mouth.

No one came to the door.

I double-checked my phone, confirming I hadn't missed a follow-up text canceling our meeting.

The front curtains were drawn, and music wafted down from the second floor. Did Mr. Jackson rent both floors? That would make more sense, I supposed, and the music explained why he hadn't heard my arrival.

I walked to the edge of the porch and looked along the side of the home. An exterior staircase stretched up to the second floor. Maybe there was an upstairs neighbor.

After another long beat of waiting, I steeled my nerves and opened the storm door so I could use the large brass knocker.

Before my fingers reached the lion's ring, a slap of something warm and gooey hit my head and splattered over my shoulders.

I screamed and a plastic bucket hit the floorboards near my feet with a hearty bounce. Sludge splashed onto my tennis shoes, calves and dress hem.

I screamed some more. Partially from shock. Mostly from outrage. It had only taken a moment for me to identify the thick sweet-scented content as maple syrup, warmed by the sun and speckled with gnats and flies that had found the bucket before me.

A feral growl ripped from my core, and I turned back to the door. I pounded with clenched fists, preparing to launch myself at Mr. Yoder and take whatever punishment the local police delivered for the assault.

The bucket rocked back and forth while I fumed at the closed door, fists falling to my sides. Wide black marks along the bucket's side pulled me to the floorboards, and I lifted the bucket with trembling hands. Someone had written four words on the plastic in sharp, angled letters.

## STOP PUSHING YOUR LUCK

"Hey," an unfamiliar voice called. The music inside had gone quiet, and a man several years younger than me appeared on the lawn beside the porch. "Are you okay, dude?"

I wiped syrup-soaked hair away from my face with sticky hands. "No," I said, feeling my bottom lip begin to tremble. "I am not okay!"

"What happened?"

I explained through gritted teeth and falling tears while he dialed the police.

A few moments later, he urged me to sit on the porch steps. "I'm Jace," he said, keeping his distance on the lawn. "I rent the second floor, and I heard you knocking."

I swallowed repeatedly, willing myself not to cry harder.

"Mr. J spends his days on campus," he said. "He's never here at this time. Do you want me to wait for the police with you?"

I shook my head. "No. I'll be okay."

He seemed relieved and turned to go.

"Jace?"

He leaned back in my direction. "What's up?"

"Which campus?"

"Community college. North Elm and Acorn Lane."

A cruiser appeared on the street, moving slowly in our direction, and Jace disappeared.

Apparently Dirk Yoder had accepted my request to speak by text this morning, then set up the syrup threat on his way to school.

It was a mean and dumb thing to do, because I was telling.

Officer Anthony rose from the car with a hand on one hip. "Really?" she said, scanning my ridiculous appearance.

I couldn't see myself as completely as she could, but I'd dared a peek in the window's reflection, and my look wasn't good.

"Dirk Yoder invited me over." I handed her my phone with our exchanged texts on the screen.

She scanned the content, then searched my eyes.

"He asked if I was still coming," I said, though she'd just read it for herself. It was the part troubling me most. "I thought he was waiting for me."

She shook her head. "All right. Let me collect the evidence, and I'll take you home."

I batted my eyes, fighting tears of humiliation. I was helpless to wipe them if they fell. My hands were still sticky from the syrup, even though I'd wiped both against my dress until they were dry.

I stood when she returned with the bucket and some syrup in evidence bags.

"How about that ride?" she asked.

I shook my head.

"Well, I can't leave you here like that." She waved to my syrup-spattered self. "You'll attract every bug in the state and need an ambulance."

A few flying things had already collected on the ruined fabric.

I considered throwing myself into the river rather than forcing the next words from my mouth, but given the day I was having, I'd probably run into a bear and be eaten.

"Can you take me to Laurelwood?"


Mama met me on the large turnaround driveway beside the fountain. I'd called to let her know I was on my way and had gotten a ride. She thanked Officer Anthony, then reached for me, before pulling back with a grimace. "What on earth!"

"It's a long story," I said. "Care if I use the shower before tea?"

Her expression of shock would've been comical if bugs hadn't started to buzz around my syrupy head. "I insist," she said. "Constance!"

Mama's house manager, a buttoned-up mouse of a woman in her thirties appeared a moment later, having clearly been waiting just inside the door. Constance was my age when she'd come on board as the house manager. I'd left for college shortly afterward and rarely saw her these last eight years, but she'd barely changed. If I didn't know she was twenty-six when she came to Laurelwood, I might assume she was that age today. A testament to her constitution. My mother could cause gray hair and wrinkles on a rock.

"Good," Mama said. "There you are." She reached for me, then withdrew once more. "Please take my daughter to her room and see that she has everything she needs to... fix this. Then, take her things to the laundry and tell Julia to prepare our lunch while Louisa bathes."

"Yes, Mrs. Eggers." Constance nodded, hands clasped before her. She turned amused eyes to mine. "Welcome home, Ms. Eggers."

I followed Constance into the house while my mother

huffed and harrumphed behind us, muttering about my arrival in a police car. I'd tried to make myself small in the back, hoping no one we passed would recognize me, but countless people had seen the cruiser headed to Laurelwood. And that wasn't good either.

Constance waited at the door for me to remove my shoes, then led me over the marble foyer floor to the sweeping staircase that wound upward to the next floor.

Mama closed the large wooden door and watched as I made my ascent.

I wasn't convinced my shoes would be there when I got back.

"I expect an explanation when you're done looking like the inside of a beehive," Mama said. "Including the name of who else was involved in whatever this is."

"It's syrup," I said.

The corners of Constance's mouth twitched as she made the turn toward my room at the top of the stairs. Her light brown hair was wound into a tight chignon at the base of her neck. A blush-colored blouse, a black skirt and pumps completed the look. Simple diamond-stud earrings graced her ears, and a set of thin golden chains rested against her collarbone. She was the picture of quiet elegance.

The sound of Mama's heels clicking away helped my shoulders slide away from my ears.

Constance stopped at the linen closet outside my room and collected a stack of fluffy white towels. She selected a terry cloth robe with a large cursive letter E embroidered on the lapel, then a pair of matching slippers.

I opened the double doors to my suite and inhaled the fruity scents of my youth. Citrus body sprays and berry-themed lotions permeated the walls, curtains and bedding. I was sure the ghost of Louisa Past was just inside my closet, chewing wads of gum and hiding from her nanny. Sixteen-year-old me was probably perfecting her winged eye-liner at the lighted vanity mirror or climbing down the trellis outside my window to meet a boy.

"Ms. Eggers?" Constance asked.

"Sorry." I squinted, falling back to the present with an unexpected tug in my heart. "I was just thinking of my life here before college."

She opened the doors to my bathroom and set the towels on the countertop before dropping the slippers on the floor. She hung the robe on a brass hook and motioned to my walk-in shower, then to my jetted tub. "Soak or shower?"

The tub called to me, but it wasn't the right tool for this job. "Shower," I said, pointing a finger at the coating of syrup in my hair.

Her mouth twitched again, but she didn't smile. "Of course." She started the water and checked the bottles of products in my caddy. All my favorites. All full. "Life before college was nice?" she asked, looking slightly embarrassed by the personal question.

I suspected she hadn't meant to voice the words. "Very." By all comparisons, my life at Laurelwood had been enchanted. I'd been a beloved princess in a gilded cage. I just hadn't noticed the bars until high school. Once I'd known they were there, I couldn't think of anything other than getting out.

She nodded, a small apologetic grin curving her lips. "I'll wait outside the door for your things."

"Thank you." I set my backpack on the counter and slid out of the sticky dress. I folded it inside out to keep the worst of the syrup contained. I donned the robe and dragged off my socks and underthings, then passed the ensemble out.

A moment later, the doors to my room closed, and I sat on the shower bench, letting the steam and scalding drops wash away my tears.

## CHAPTER THIRTEEN

*I* strode into the dining room with my back straight and chin up, as Mama preferred. I'd redressed in the contents of a garment bag I'd found draped across my bed.

The dress was ivory, modest and tea length with an off-the-shoulder neckline. The design reminded me of something from another era. Maybe that was why Mama had chosen it for me. She preferred more structured, modern looks, but this was exactly my style. The bodice was stretchy but clingy, and the skirt flowed freely over my hips from the waist. If I spun, the material flared out and spun with me. I'd experimented several times in front of my mirror before coming downstairs.

"Louisa," Mama said, spotting me from her place in the kitchen. "You look lovely. Do you like it?" She motioned to me from head to toe, including the new ivory sandals in her question.

"Yes. Everything's beautiful. And a perfect fit. How did you know the right size?"

"A mother knows. What did you do about new under things?"

I stifled a groan and kept my voice even when I answered. "I found everything I needed in my dresser." Everything I'd left behind after college had been washed, dried, folded and left waiting for me. Just in case I ever dropped in for a visit and needed hot-pink polka-dotted panties or a rainbow-striped pushup bra. "I can't believe you kept all of that."

Her brow rose in surprise. "It's all yours. What would I do? Throw it out?" she asked. "Aren't you glad I didn't?"

"Touché."

"Do you always keep dresses on hand in my size?" I asked.

"I try," she said. "When I see something I think is perfect for you, I usually pick it up. I miss shopping with you, you know."

A ball of emotion rose in my throat. I'd enjoyed our days together too. I even missed them from time to time. And Mama.

Mama passed into the dining room and motioned for me to sit. "Now, explain the syrup."

A table for fourteen was set for two on one end. Mama took her seat at the head, and I sat on her right side, deciding how to answer.

An antique chandelier hung from the ceiling, ten feet above the table. Cherry wood wainscoting rose from the polished wooden floorboards to the chair rail at my hip. Floral wallpaper climbed upward from there, stretching to reach the crown molding where it lined the ceiling. Heavy blue curtains were pinned back at each of two windows. A massive hutch and sideboard stood between them. The furniture had been a wedding gift from my great-grandparents to my grandparents, then passed down with the house to my mother. The china and silverware on the table were significantly older than that.

Mama set her napkin over her lap and motioned for the service to begin with a bend of two fingers. "The syrup," she nudged, fixing her eyes on me.

I took a deep breath and told my tale. There wasn't any sense in hiding details. She'd know it all soon enough. At least providing the facts up front would help her to set the gossips straight when they came calling.

Mama listened closely as small bowls of cool strawberry soup and salads fresh from the garden were served.

I took a sip from the tea set before me, then finished the story.

"I suppose it's good to know some things haven't changed," she said, her expression carefully bland.

"What's that supposed to mean?" It wasn't as if I'd had murderers taunting me all my life. Thankfully, the routine threats had only begun in recent months. And hopefully they'd soon be over.

Mama waved a dismissive hand, then lowered it to her lap. "Only that you're still the same young lady who left home for college, then again to make a life in Meadow Town. You dress differently and live elsewhere, but you're still you."

"It's Meadowbrook," I corrected, knowing she'd intentionally misspoken. "And of course I'm still me. Who else would I be?"

She shrugged, then lifted a spoon to her soup. "I'm not sure. I suppose you're figuring it out."

I waited for the dig that didn't follow.

"You never could tolerate a secret of any kind," she continued. "You were the first of your friends to find out about Santa, assuming you ever believed at all. You found your holiday and birthday gifts no matter how well I hid them, and you spent a good portion of your teen years upset with someone for lying."

"Someone was always lying," I said, dipping into my soup.

"It drove me nuts."

"You worked for your high school and college newspapers," she said. "You chose research work for your senior-year thesis, when everyone else created a passion project. Private investigation is on par for you, I suppose. And this case hit home, considering Mr. Flint fell on you when he died."

I bit the insides of my cheeks. She wasn't wrong, but she also wasn't freaking out as I'd expected. And apparently she'd heard all about the details of Mr. Flint's death. "You're not mad?"

"Oh, I'm furious," she assured. "I'm also well-aware of how effective telling you to knock this off will be." She set her spoon aside and dabbed the corners of her mouth with a linen napkin. "So, since I obviously cannot stop you, how can I keep you safe?"

I blinked. "You want to help me?"

"Of course. Any chance I can convince you to stay here while you blunder around?"

"Mama," I said, confused by the twisted notions and my competing emotions. I wanted to insist I didn't blunder, but given the condition I'd arrived in, I assumed the argument was weak. "I'm safe at home."

"You would be safer here."

"Maybe," I conceded, but I couldn't agree to that just yet. "I'm more concerned I'll be taken to jail than afraid of the petty threats."

"First of all, no threat against my daughter is ever petty. And secondly, I'll be reaching out to the police this afternoon. They should know I've spoken to my attorney, and they should proceed with caution where you're concerned. How close are you and the Irish fellow?"

It took a minute for my brain to catch up from the lightning-fast subject change. "Do you mean Eli?"

"Of course I mean Eli. Do you know another Irishman?"

I bit my lip against a smart retort. "You called him a Scot the last time he came up."

"And you said he's Irish."

I forced my shoulders back, feeling the frustration mount. "Why are you asking about him again?"

"He's former military, is he not?" She lifted her fork and moved on to her salad. "He could be useful."

I frowned. "We don't talk about our pasts. Why do you think he was in the military? And how is that useful?"

"Private security," she said. "I need to know if he can protect you or if I should hire a bodyguard."

A sudden laugh bubbled out of me, drawing Mama's warning eyes. "Do not hire a bodyguard."

She pushed the veggies around her plate while I made short work of my salad, imagining Eli with an ear piece and speaking into his watch.

When I finished, Mama lifted her chin. "I could use your help around here. Not all the time. Not enough to ruin the life you're building out there in the forest but whenever you can spare a few hours. I could use them."

I bit my lip against the agitation that always came when she mentioned my new life as if I'd run off to live in a blanket fort. "I don't understand. You have a full staff here. What do you need help with?"

"Everything."

"Care to narrow that down?"

She huffed an exaggerated sigh. "The estate, the gardens, the living museum. Public relations. Guest relations. Charity affiliations. Do I really need to go on?"

"No." I shook my head. "I know it's a lot. I guess I'm surprised you need the added hands. You've never had any trouble finding enough help before." Though she had recently hired Mary, who would be absolutely terrible as a staff member facing the public on a daily basis. Maybe Mama was losing her instinct.

She cleared her throat, piquing my attention. She never fussed or fretted visibly. And she never cleared her throat. "It's come to my attention that your father did more around here than I'd realized. Without him, I'm spread too thin, and the last few years have become increasingly difficult for me."

"Can't he help from the cabin?" I wasn't sure what Dad did with himself these days, since he rarely reached out to me, and I returned his calls less often than Mama's. There weren't any hard feelings between us, but I didn't like that he'd walked out. A mutual split? Fine. But running away under the guise of work trips for longer and longer periods, until he stopped coming home at all was despicable, and I wasn't over it. Even if Mama was. As far as I knew, their divorce wasn't final. "Surely he would step in and do what he can from wherever he is."

Mama's expression soured. "Just think about it," she said, ignoring my mention of Dad. "Please."

"Okay."

I remembered in the next heartbeat that I had a question for her as well. "Do you know if Sophia Cardiff started selling her designs to more than one person?"

Mama's brows furrowed. "Of course not. Why? Are you interested in a new bag? We can make a trip together. My treat. Anything you'd like. Constance can drive."

"No. Thank you," I said. "But I was wondering about a particular purse I saw at my shop. I saw it again a day or two later, and the owner claimed she hadn't been at Souffle the Day. It was odd."

Mama's brow puckered. "Either one of the two bags was a knock off or the woman you spoke with is lying. Sophia will never create the same design twice. She's an artist, not a conveyor belt for tchotchkes."

Exactly what I thought she'd say.

An hour later, I paused in the doorway to hug her. "Thank you for taking care of me today."

She slid a palm down my arm from shoulder to elbow. "The police dropped you off covered in syrup. What was I supposed to do? Turn you away?"

"I'm not just talking about today."

Emotion bloomed in her eyes, and she stroked my hair. "I will always do everything in my power to keep you safe and well. Occasionally against your will if necessary."

A chuckle rose from my core, and I couldn't help feeling as if we'd put a crack in the wall between us.

"Oh." She lifted a finger and ducked into the house. She returned a moment later with her cell phone and tapped the screen. My phone dinged. "I've sent you the information you'll need to reach Sophia if you want to ask her about that handbag. Or if you decide you'd like one of your own. Tell her to add it to my account."

"Thank you, Mama." I kissed her cheek. "I don't need a two thousand dollar purse, but I appreciate the offer."

"Get something for Thelma then or Jill," she said, smiling once more. "I hear she's about to be a bride."

"Invitations are on the way."

Constance pulled a black Hummer into the drive near the fountain and idled while I hugged Mama goodbye.

"Don't be a stranger," she called as I bounced down the steps toward my waiting ride.

"I won't," I promised. "I'll be back soon to help."

Pride rose in her eyes, and my heart soared.

Whatever happened, I'd always have a place here with Mama.

Assuming I wasn't in jail.

## CHAPTER FOURTEEN

*C*onstance pointed the SUV toward Meadowbrook, and I dialed Sophia's number, hoping she'd have a moment to speak with me soon. I shamelessly name-dropped Mama to tip the scales in my favor.

She hummed a low note. "All right, darling. C'mon."

"Change of plans," I told Constance.

She glanced curiously as I gave her the new address but didn't complain or ask questions. I was certain she'd report back to my mother the moment I was out of her sight, but that was okay.

I hurried along the walk to a gray clapboard home. The door was black with a frosted oval window trimmed in white. Sophia's last name curled across the etched glass.

*Cardiff*

I let myself in and was met with the supple scent of leather. My mind immediately filled with images of new riding boots, crops and saddles.

Deep mahogany and cherry shelves lined the walls, showcasing Sophia's newest creations. A large round table at the shop's center boasted framed photos and articles featuring her work in magazines, on television and in movies.

"Darling," she called, her smoky voice taking me back a dozen years. "There you are. Come in. How are you? What can I do?" She approached me with open arms, and I bent to hug her.

Sophia was small and narrow with rich brown skin and straight black hair that hung in an angled bob along her chin. A rectangle of thick bangs rested across her forehead.

"Hello, Mrs. Cardiff. Thank you for seeing me."

"Of course." She stepped back and motioned me to a broad design desk along the far wall. "Sit. Let's talk."

"Thank you."

She examined me with wide brown eyes. "You don't look like someone who's been living in the woods. Was it a façade?"

"Beg your pardon?"

"A ruse." She circled a wrist as she took the seat beside me. "A coverup."

"For what?"

"Anything. A torrid affair. Time spent in rehab. A secret love child."

I grimaced. "No. None of that. And I don't live in the woods. I live in Meadowbrook."

She processed, eyes pensive. "No wonder your mother doesn't like to talk about it."

I inhaled deeply through my nose and sat taller. "Meadowbrook is a lovely, wholesome community. If you ever want to visit, I'd be honored to show you around. You might find inspiration there, not that you're in need of inspiration," I added quickly. "You seem to have the tap on new ideas."

Sophia crossed her short legs. The flared bottoms of her

black dress pants rose, exposing her signature C embroidered on dark dress socks.

"Do you ever make two of the same designs?" I asked. "I know that's not your general policy, but I assume there are exceptions to every rule."

Maybe a pair of women requested matching bags or she'd unwittingly made two strikingly similar purses.

She wrinkled her features, as if I'd insulted her. "No."

"Never? Not for a special occasion or at a customer's request?"

"Never."

I gave her the rundown on why I wanted to know, then added, "I only saw the bag for a moment the first time, so I suppose it's possible I was mistaken."

Sophia lifted her chin, curiosity piqued. "Describe, please."

"Hot-pink," I said quickly, before she changed her mind. "Medium-sized, structured with broad straps and two yellow pompoms." I stopped myself short of saying the accessories looked like popcorn, preferring to see what she came up with instead.

"Ah." She leaned forward, resting clasped hands on the table between us. "This is about Tina Flint." Mischief glinted in her eyes. "Not a coincidence after what happened to her husband at your café." She shifted, uncrossing and recrossing her legs. "You think you saw her there because you saw her purse. She says it wasn't her. Why lie?"

"Exactly," I answered, wondering belatedly if Sophia had a history of gossip. She certainly had access. Women spent hours in her company, designing and shopping for the perfect signature handbag. Maybe a few men too. Creating custom versions of anything required a level of intimacy and rapport that could easily lead to sharing secrets, personal or otherwise.

Sophia steepled her short fingers. "Let's make a trade. Then we'll talk about my designs."

"What kind of trade?"

"I need feathers. You still raise chickens in the forest?"

"I breed Polish hens in Meadowbrook," I clarified. "Yes. They're blue-ribbon winners and frequently featured in related magazines and articles. Free range. No hormones. Naturally fed." The spiel fell from my lips out of habit. Typically anyone asking about my hens was interested in purchasing them or they were being judged at an event.

She wrinkled her nose. "I don't want to eat them. I just want their feathers."

"For what?" I asked, not that it mattered. There were enough loose feathers in my life to outfit her in new pillows and bedding for a lifetime. Possibly a few puffy coats as well.

"Ah ah ah," she said, looking like the cat who ate the canary. "That's a design secret. You'll have to come back and see." She tapped a nearby folder, indicating her feathery plan would soon be included inside.

I tucked that in the back of my mind for later and nodded. "Okay. Deal."

Sophia pulled a thick binder from a stack on the table's corner and tabbed to a section marked PINK. She spun the book to face me. "I keep a photo inventory of all my work so I won't come too close to replication. Sometimes clients see something they want and ask me to design it, but I never repeat."

I turned the pages quickly. "Do you get many requests for hot pink?"

"Not in four decades."

I nodded, chewing my lip as I searched for the bag in question. "Here." I stopped on an image of Mrs. Flint's bag. "This one."

"I made only one," she confirmed.

So, Tina Flint had been present the night her husband died and lied about it. Why would she do that?

Sophia watched me, seeming to have more to say. "Do you have any other questions you'd like me to answer? For the sake of our trade?"

I sensed I should choose my words carefully. Sophia was an elite business woman, and being labeled as a gossip could ruin her. Perhaps she saw our trade agreement as an appropriate reason to share information. Regardless, I was a dog on this case, and she'd thrown a bone. "Is there anything else I should know about the owner of this purse?"

"Probably. But I don't know her well. We only did business once."

I nodded, rethinking my question. "Was there anything unusual about the experience?"

She shook her head.

"Did you know Mr. Flint?" I tried.

Another head shake.

"Have you heard anything about him I should know? The police think I killed him, but I didn't," I added before she shook her head again. "The real killer is taunting and threatening me, so I really need to figure out who that is and get them arrested before I wind up like Mr. Flint." I'd realized while shampooing syrup from my hair, that it didn't make much sense for Dirk Yoder to incriminate himself by leaving a threat on his own porch. Sadly, I didn't know what to make of that either. If it wasn't Mr. Yoder, then who'd sent the texts?

Her red lips parted. "You're being threatened?" A flash of fear and protectiveness colored her tone and hardened her features. "How so?"

"Warning messages, flat tires, strange gifts and notes. Then I got a bucket of syrup dumped on my head when I visited Dirk Yoder this morning. Mr. Yoder was in charge of the town's website before Mr. Flint took over."

Sophia squared her shoulders. "Do you have any questions about that?"

"About Mr. Yoder?" I guessed. Unless she meant the syrup.

She waited. For a proper question, I presumed.

"Do you know anything about Dirk Yoder or the town website that I should know?" I asked. "Something that might help me figure this out?"

"I had lunch with the ladies a few days ago on the patio outside The Bistro," she said, pushing a length of bobbed hair behind one ear. "The morning after Mr. Flint died. Dirk Yoder was passing the café on the sidewalk, talking on his phone. He seemed very happy. He said he couldn't wait to get started revamping the town website. It didn't fit his vision, and he planned to change it back to the way it was meant to be."

I worked to keep my expression neutral. "Interesting."

"Agreed. You might want to talk to him, darling. But you didn't hear any of that from me."

Sophia snapped the book shut and returned it to the pile, then stood, apparently finishing our chat.

"Thank you," I said. "I'll try again, but he wasn't home when I stopped by earlier. His neighbor said he was at school. Apparently he attends the community college."

"Dirk is a professor. Not a student."

I processed that a moment. After meeting Mr. Yoder's neighbor, I'd wondered about his age. The community college had a diverse population, and it wasn't uncommon to see retirees taking classes with teenagers. If Dirk Yoder had been young, it would've been easier to imagine someone in charge giving his job to Mr. Flint, who was older and presumably more experienced. "Does he teach English?"

Maybe something techie? Or marketing and communication?

Sophia leaned closer, lips pinched. "Dirk teaches criminal justice."

Did that mean he knew how to get away with murder?

CHAPTER FIFTEEN

*I* called Mary to see if the community truck was available. I was fully capable of walking, and I knew Constance would return for me if I called her, but neither of those options felt right.

Thankfully, Mary answered her phone and arrived at the Corner Cup before I had time to finish my bottle of water. She leaned across the bench seat to shove the passenger door open when I reached the sidewalk.

We were in motion before I could buckle my seatbelt.

"What's going on?" she asked. "Those aren't your clothes, and why weren't you at your mom's place? Did you walk all the way here from there? Did you tell her I sent you?"

I rolled my head against the back of the seat to face her. "Are you ready for all those answers?"

She frowned. "I asked, didn't I?"

"Okay." I unloaded all the details of my day.

"So, the guy who started the town's blog teaches criminal justice at the collegiate level, and he was kicked off the website job he started so Flint could take over?" She paused.

"I hope you pushed him to the top of your suspect list. That sounds incriminating as heck."

I nodded. "Yeah. Then there's Flint's wife. She gave me weird vibes when we spoke the other day, and I can't understand why she would lie about being at Souffle the Day when he died. Unless she had something to do with his death. She knew about his allergy, and she has a temper."

"I have a temper," Mary said. "I'm not a killer." She drove in silence for a few beats, then turned to face me again. "Dirk Yoder set a bucket of syrup on his door and let it dump on you?"

"Yep."

"What is he? Some black-and-white cartoon character or that kid from *Home Alone*?"

I snorted. The attack was peculiar for sure, and I couldn't understand why he'd invite me over just to threaten me. But if he wasn't the killer, why was he threatening me?

"And you agreed to go back and help your mom?" Mary asked.

"Yep." I hoped I wouldn't regret it.

"What do you think the purse lady wants feathers for?"

"She didn't say, but I could use help collecting them," I said hopefully.

"Jeez," Mary mock-complained, making a show of hitting the turn signal and taking the lane into Meadowbrook. "I haven't even finished doing the last thing you asked of me."

"Thank you for picking me up. Would you like to stay for tea?"

Mary leaned over the steering wheel, eyes fixed on something in the distance. "No thanks. I hate being a third wheel, and it looks as if you already have company."

I followed her attention to my cottage as it rose from the trees. A man was seated in the rocker outside my door. Thelma stood on his lap. "Eli."

"He's become your hunky, brooding shadow the last couple months," Mary said. "Anything going on there I should know about?"

My cheeks heated. "We're becoming friends, I think."

Mary smiled. "I heard you're getting married."

I barked a laugh. "That was an unfortunate misunderstanding. Murray made assumptions when I asked him to borrow plants for Jack and Jill's wedding."

"If you say so. But having Eli Fogle as a shadow certainly can't be a hardship. I'd hit a bear with a rolling pin if it got that guy's attention."

I laughed, and she turned onto my driveway.

I climbed out with a grin. "You sure you don't want to stay?"

She gave Eli a long, appreciative look before turning back to me. "I think I'll head over to my place and collect some feathers for you. Give your new friend some variety. Maybe I'll check on Dimitri at the stables later. Sometimes he takes his shirt off when he's breaking a new horse."

Word around Meadowbrook was that Dimitri returned home from four years in the military to find his girlfriend involved with his best friend. He'd packed his bags in search of someplace to start over. Now he trained and boarded horses.

"Enjoy," I said, patting the truck's hood as she shifted into reverse.

"Don't need luck," she called. "I'm only going for the show."

I went to meet Eli on my porch and stroked the puffy feathers on Thelma's tiny head. "Fancy seeing you here," I said. "Everything okay?"

*Bawk-ah!*

"Not you, silly. Your human chair."

Eli set Thelma aside and stretched onto his feet, towering

over me. "Just checking in. Thelma greeted me, so I sat to say hello."

"I'm sure she appreciated it. It was hard to leave her, but she was better off staying here than going to my mother's with me."

I wasn't even sure what would get syrup off of feathers.

"You went to see your mother?" Eli asked, a note of approval in his tone.

"Yep." I unlocked my door and tipped my head. "Want to come in and hear about it?"

He rubbed his palms against his pantlegs, then nodded and followed.

I led him to the kitchen, realizing I hadn't eaten since lunch with Mama, and I'd been too shaken to enjoy the soup and salad properly. "Are you hungry?" I asked, turning to catch Eli looking more shy and uncomfortable than I'd ever seen him. "I'm starving."

"Actually, yeah." He cleared his throat, and I glanced back at him. "I was coming by to see if you had dinner plans. I thought we could get something together."

"How do you feel about grilling and chilling? I need to spend some time with Thelma and the other animals. We can eat on the patio, and when the sun sets, you could build another fire. If you decided to stay that long."

Eli grinned. "You don't have any more plans today?"

"Nope." And if I was being completely honest, Eli was the person I'd most like to spend more time with.

I leaned against my kitchen island and told myself not to fidget. "What do you say?"

His hazel eyes danced. "It's a date."

An hour later, we sat on my patio, watching the animals and finishing our meals. I'd grilled veggies from the garden and a pair of bass from a nearby stream. The relentless heat of the day had given way to a more manageable evening, complete with gentle breeze and hope of rain.

Eli rose with our empty plates and moved toward the back door. "Let me take these to the sink, then I'll start a fire."

I gathered our glasses and followed. "I'll pour refills."

Inside, he rinsed the dishes and watched as I poured fresh tea over new cubes of ice. "Thanks for dinner," he said. "It's nice to have someone to share meals with."

"Thanks for joining me. I could get used to this little routine." My cheeks burned at my boldness, but it pleased instead of embarrassed me. I'd meant the words, and appreciated the relationship blooming between us.

Eli set our plates onto the drying rack, and I realized he'd washed them.

"Hey, stop," I said. "You don't have to do that. You're my guest. I'll clean up later."

"You made dinner," he argued, meeting me at the island. "You opened your home to me, even after the day you had. The least I can do is make things a little easier."

"What do you know about my day?" I asked.

We'd talked about my visit with Mama, but the conversation had slipped into shared summer memories from there, then to nostalgia brought on by lightning bugs.

"I ran into Officer Anthony while I was out delivering firewood," he said. "She filled me in."

I shook my head as we moved back onto the patio with our drinks. Eli lowered onto the chair beside mine.

"How much did she tell you?" I supposed a run-in with Officer Anthony explained why he'd come to check on me, then decided to wait on my porch. And possibly why he was hanging out for the evening again.

"Enough to worry me," he said.

I groaned. "You'd think cops would have better things to do than gossip. She must think I'm a public nuisance."

He smiled.

"I can't believe you knew about the syrup and still let me talk about Mama's plans to get me on the payroll." I grimaced. "How long did you talk with Officer Anthony?"

"A while."

A strange pinch of jealousy caught me off guard. I didn't care whom Eli spoke to. So, what was my problem?

"Louisa?"

His sincere hazel gaze met mine, and I realized the pang I'd felt was a desire to know him better and for him to know me, as well. Not jealousy, but longing.

"Tell me everything," he said. "I want to hear it all from you."

A slow smile spread over my face as Eli's words landed on my heart.

He wanted to know me too.

"I planned to talk with Dirk Yoder at his place this morning," I began, and Eli listened carefully as I unloaded the details.

When I finished, he nodded, expression carefully blank. "Well, if you're going anywhere tomorrow, I'd like to be your chauffeur."

## CHAPTER SIXTEEN

*E*li picked me up in the community truck the next morning. "No Thelma?" he asked, flicking his attention from me to the yard alongside my home.

"Not today." I'd waffled over whether to take her with me yesterday, then thanked my lucky stars I hadn't. I didn't want to choose differently and regret it today.

I buckled up and arranged the skirt of my red with white pinstripes dress around my legs. The scoop neck was broad, exposing a wide swath of skin, and the material hung loosely from my hips, making it one of my cooler dresses, and first choice when temperatures were expected to tip the scale.

Eli wore a simple gray t-shirt and blue jeans with work boots. His red hair was dark and damp, and the scents of soap and shampoo filled the cab.

I wet my lips in delight.

"Where to?" he asked, swinging an arm across the back of the seat and twisting for a look over his shoulder.

My heart rate kicked up. Why was that move so darn titillating?

He reversed out of my drive, then turned expectant eyes on me.

"The community college, please."

We drove through town at a crawl, moving along with morning commuters. I wondered how many of our fellow travelers were also on their ways to school.

I watched as downtown inched by, then as the roads grew wide and curvy, leading us away from the congestion.

Eli was unusually quiet, maybe as lost in thought as I was. I wished I knew what was on his mind, but my own concerns kept me from asking.

According to the website, the college campus was big. I had no idea how to find Dirk Yoder once we arrived. What if today was his day off or if he didn't come in until later? I supposed, if we knew for sure, we could pass our time wandering the grounds. I'd never been to the community college before, but I'd always heard nice things.

"It's been a while since I've driven out this way," Eli said. "Not since I first came to town."

"Did you go to school here? I thought you went to college in Virginia." I guessed he could have taken extra classes after moving here. I tried to recall the details of Eli's arrival in Meadowbrook, but he'd been solitary and unwelcoming at first. He'd accepted casseroles with a nod. Waves and smiles with a frown and frequently left his property to hike and camp for days at a time.

I'd been drawn to his rugged mysteriousness from the start. Funny that after spending some time around him, I was even more attracted to his patient heart and gentle soul than the package it came in.

Eli had blossomed in Meadowbrook. He'd made friends throughout our community and the town. He had a long list of regular customers who bought his firewood and ordered everything from horseshoes to personalized rings made at his blacksmith shop. Folks always spoke to him on sight, and he responded in kind.

I wasn't sure if something happened to change his responses or if he'd just needed space upon arrival—needed time to heal from… something. I supposed we all had our share of things to process before we found our ways.

"No, no school here. You remember correctly," he said, answering a question I'd nearly forgotten asking. "But I make a habit of knowing my surroundings, so I explored the town at length after my move."

"You spent time on campus just because it's part of Cromwell?"

"I spent time everywhere for that reason."

Huh. "So what did you study in college?"

"Psychology."

*Unexpected, but interesting.*

Eli slid his eyes to mine. "What's that face? Not a fan of psychology?"

"I don't know. I pegged you for studying How to be the Ultimate Outdoorsman or maybe a Wilderness Survival Specialist," I teased.

He laughed. "If either of those was real, I could probably teach the classes. Nature, I understand. People are peculiar. And a little disturbing."

*We were in agreement there.*

He settled the truck in a lot designated for visitors, then unfastened his seatbelt. "Ready?"

I scanned the meandering people with tired faces and massive bookbags. "Yep."

Unexpected chills rolled over my skin in waves as we approached the Student Center. I rubbed my palms roughly against my arms, attempting to scrub the feeling away.

"Everything okay?" Eli asked.

I nodded, a little unsure. No one seemed to be paying us

any attention, so I shook off the heebie-jeebies and opened the large glass door. "According to the website, the administration office is on the second floor."

We climbed a set of floating steps with a glass half wall as a railing, dodging hurried students and a few folks I assumed were professors.

I headed for the large blue counter at the end of the upstairs hallway, but Eli hung back, examining a display of brochures on the wall.

"May I help you?" A young woman with bright-blue eyes and gas-blue hair stared across the counter at me.

"Yes, hi." I admired her sunshine-yellow cardigan, which partly covered a t-shirt with a cartoon bird's nest and the words Have an Eggs-cellent Day beneath. I was certain she wore the shirt ironically, but now that I knew it existed, I wanted one too. "I'm hoping to speak with a professor here. Dirk Yoder."

She pressed her lips together. "I'm sorry. I don't have access to the professors' schedules. Have you tried his office? Most people post their office hours on their door. You can leave a note for him to get back with you if he's out."

"Right." I nodded. "Can you remind me which office is his and how to find it? I had an appointment yesterday, and I missed him."

"You had an appointment with him yesterday, but don't know where his office is?"

"I'd planned to meet with him at his home. I'm not a student here, so I'm not familiar with the buildings."

Her expression soured, as if she thought I might be a stalker asking for a little assistance setting up my hidden cameras. "Maybe I can take your name and number and email it to him instead."

Eli moved to my side and set a brochure on the counter. "Hi. Do I need an appointment to get a tour of campus?" he asked. "I'm new to the area, and someone said this is a good place to finish my degree."

The girl's eyes widened as she took him in, and she blinked. "Hi. Yeah. For sure. I can take you."

I turned to Eli, who held the girl's eye contact as she put a little plastic sign on the counter explaining she was out. "What are you doing?"

"Taking a tour of campus," he said. "Would you like to join us?"

The girl rounded the counter to stand before Eli, hand extended. "I'm Stacy."

"Eli."

"Eli," she repeated, a little too breathlessly. She was far too young for him, not that it was any of my business.

I frowned. "Sure," I said, leaning around him to catch Stacy's eye. "I'd love to join you." Maybe I'd see Dirk Yoder while we walked. I'd seen enough online photos of him in my research. I was sure I could pick him out in a crowd.

Stacy didn't look as if she'd heard me—or cared.

Eli handed the brochure he'd been carrying to me, and I saw he'd folded it back to the current criminal justice course offerings. According to the schedule, D. Yoder taught classes from room R1120 and another room a few doors down.

I followed Stacy and Eli away from the administration office and out of the Student Center through a side door.

"What are you studying?" Stacy asked, tugging her blue hair over one shoulder and smiling shyly as she walked. "We can start the tour in the area where your classes will be."

"Law enforcement," he answered smoothly. "I plan to work for the FBI. My experience in the military, coupled with a degree, will make me a prime candidate."

She slowed to make googly eyes at him. "The FBI sounds really cool. You were in the military?"

He nodded and something dark passed in his carefully

composed expression. I thought of Mama's interest in hiring him as a bodyguard, and wondered if what he'd told Stacy was true.

"Well, thank you for your service," she said. "I like to thank our heroes when I see them."

I rolled my eyes.

Eli shot me a crazy look, and I hoped I hadn't made a gagging sound out loud.

Stacy opened the door on a red-brick building and motioned me inside. "I guess we'll start your tour here."

A statue of the scales of justice stood in the four-story foyer.

I concentrated on the room numbers as we walked the interior hallways.

Dirk Yoder wasn't teaching in either of the rooms where his name appeared on the course brochure.

Eventually, Stacy left us at the campus coffee cart, but not before telling Eli to reach out if he had any more questions or wanted a private tour around town.

I glared when he looked my way. "Seriously?"

He grinned. "She was nice."

"Dirk Yoder wasn't in either of his classrooms," I said, avoiding the subject of Eli's newest fan. "I didn't notice any long rows of professors' offices, like we had at my college."

"You want to go back inside and see if we can find them? Or maybe ask a student?"

A flash of dark hair drew my eyes to the front of the coffee cart line, and I sighed in relief. "Actually, I think he might be getting his morning cup of joe."

Eli followed my gaze to Dirk Yoder, clad in a tweed blazer and khaki pants, a messenger bag hooked over one shoulder and a cup of coffee in his hand.

I hurried in his direction before he could disappear into a crowd and get away. "Mr. Yoder," I called. "Hello," I called brightly, hoping to hide the fact I wasn't feeling particularly confident on the inside. I still hadn't decided who was behind the nasty syrup-threat, but if it was him, I could be confronting a killer. One who'd told me, repeatedly, to stop asking question.

He looked me over, then Eli. "Can I help you?"

"I hope so. I'm Louisa Eggers."

He waited politely but without a hint of recognition. His thick brows furrowed and sharp jawline tensed.

I glanced at Eli. Even if he didn't know my face, he should've known my name. Unless my earlier suspicion was right, and he hadn't been the one who'd sent me those texts. "We exchanged text messages yesterday," I prompted, overcome with memories of the calamity that had followed.

He shook his head slowly, apparently mystified.

"You invited me over to discuss Mr. Flint's death."

"No. I wouldn't do that," he said. "Anyway my phone's been missing for two days. I must've set it down somewhere and forgotten it. It's been powered off every time I've tried to track it. The battery's got to be dead by now."

As it became clear someone must have set Yoder up—unless he was a really good liar—he narrowed his eyes.

"Wait," he said. "Are you the lady who was slimed on my porch?"

I felt my expression wilt. "Guilty."

"A police officer came here to talk to me already. I wasn't even home when that happened. I was in class. She confirmed it."

"I'm not here to ask about the syrup," I said. "Do you have a minute?"

He stared, as if trying to make a deduction. "You wanted to talk about Flint's death."

I nodded. "If you don't mind."

Something tugged at his lips. Amusement? "You're the woman whose food he ate before he dropped dead."

I blanched, gaze darting through the nearby space, hoping no one had overheard.

"Yeah," he said, a grin tugging his lips. "I've got a minute to talk."

We moved toward a bench in the shadow of a massive oak tree.

Eli followed.

"So," Dirk said, clearly intrigued now. "Someone took my phone and messaged you?"

"They responded to my request to meet up. I called first, but you didn't answer, so I texted."

He nodded. "And the person invited you to my house, under the guise it was me. Then sabotaged you when you arrived."

I bit the insides of my cheeks, attempting to keep the humiliation away. "They also wrote a direct threat on the bucket holding the syrup."

Dirk looked from me to Eli. "Why a threat?"

"We were hoping you could answer that," Eli said.

Dirk sipped his coffee. "Well, it wasn't to make me seem like a suspect. Why would I use my own phone to text you and create a record of our exchange, then attack you on my porch?"

His tone implied something about all of this was ridiculous, and, possibly, so was I.

I didn't appreciate it. "I never said this person was a criminal mastermind." The last killer I'd met wasn't the sharpest stick in the forest either, and I'd learned it didn't take brains to make a mistake and want to cover your tracks. All someone needed was the right motivation. "I think someone got in over their head and panicked. And they keep panicking."

He broke into a grin. "Oh, I like you. Let's sit." He lowered onto the bench and patted the space at his side.

"I'm just trying to find out who's threatening me."

"It isn't me, and I didn't kill Flint," he said. "What else would you like to know?"

I sat, and Eli moved closer but remained standing. His guarded gaze took inventory of the scene around us.

I turned to Dirk. "How did a criminal justice professor come to start a food blog?"

He gave a soft grunt. "I have some tech knowledge and was asked to assist in the creation of the town's website. I did. Adding a blog to showcase local businesses was a no-brainer."

"You're a professor, a techie and a food critic?" I asked. "A jack of all trades?"

"I'm a professor, and my experience in forensics made me a good choice for criminal justice courses," he said. "As for the website, I pick up technology easily, and the site is basic, user-friendly. Anyone on this campus could run it too, probably half the local high school students and my grandma as well. I started the food blog because I'm human and love to eat."

Eli's shadow vanished as he turned to face us, devoured by the shadow of the tree. "You worked in forensics?"

Dirk nodded. "For a very short while."

"What happened?" I asked.

He wet his lips and looked away. "I saw something my rookie year that I will never unsee, and I knew the job wasn't for me. I quit. And those who can't do, teach, right?" He forced a smile that didn't reach his eyes.

"So what happened?" I asked. "Why did Flint take over?"

"When the town council saw the food blog was getting a lot of traffic from outside town, they wanted someone with more experience to take over. Flint was older, he had more life experience, and friends on the council. But he wasn't any more qualified than I am."

I cocked a brow. "Did that make you angry?"

Dirk laughed. "Yeah, at the council, not Flint."

"Are you sure?"

He sobered. "Listen. If I killed someone, you'd never find a single clue that led you to me. That's a guarantee."

I shivered at the menace in his tone.

"Now if you'll excuse me," he said, rising and nodding his goodbyes. "I have class in twenty minutes."

Eli moved to my side.

"That was quite a mood swing," I said, replaying the exchange in small mental pieces. What had I said that made Dirk rush away?

Eli crossed his arms and stared at the retreating professor. "I think you hit a nerve."

$\mathcal{M}$ary frowned as she drove me back into town the next afternoon. Eli had work to catch up on and couldn't chauffeur me, but I had an emergency.

Thankfully, the pickup and Mary were available.

"And that's all she said?" Mary asked, as abashed as I was about an unexpected call I'd received moments before panic-dialing her.

My grip tightened on the basket of eggs balanced on my lap. "Yep."

She glanced my way. "Officer Anthony told you to come to the police station in an hour without telling you why?"

I nodded, eyes fixed to the horizon, my mind and body strangely detached.

"What do you think it means?" she asked. "Do you think it's about the soy she found in your refrigerator? Or what happened to you at Dirk Yoder's house?"

My chest tightened. "I'm just hoping she doesn't arrest me when I walk through the door." Then who would find Mr. Flint's real killer? Surely, not the police. They'd believe the case was closed. "That's why I wanted to bring the eggs to

The Weathervane now and make a proper introduction between you and Mrs. Carin. Just in case."

Mary gave me a sideways look but didn't speak.

"Once the two of you exchange contact information, you can stay in touch and sell your eggs to her without me in the middle. I don't want you to be without work if I'm thrown in jail."

Mary piloted the pickup into the busy lot outside The Weathervane and parked. "You aren't going to be arrested. Their evidence is circumstantial at best, and any attorney on earth could get the charges dropped."

"What if you're wrong?" I asked, hating the small quake in my voice. From where I was sitting, the evidence felt like an anvil hanging over my head.

"If I'm wrong, I'll bake you a cake with a file in it."

I snorted, and Mary climbed out, taking her basket of eggs with her.

She waited for me to meet her at the tailgate, then we moved through the parking lot together. I held the café's door for her to pass.

"If I'm wrong, I'll pick up where you left off," she said, circling back to our stilted conversation. "I'll carry out your investigation until the truth is found and you're set free."

I pressed a palm to my chest. "Thank you."

She rolled her eyes. "Don't get all sappy. I don't like people or make friends easily. You wore me down, and now we're cool. I don't want to start over with someone else."

I grinned. "You like me."

"Stop it."

"You like me," I sang.

"Shut up or I'll testify against you."

I laughed, and her lips quirked, struggling against a smile.

The Weathervane was housed inside a revamped barn on an old farm. The barn was two stories and red, trimmed in black and white. The hay lofts had been removed to reveal sky-high rafters inside, from which lanterns and bistro lights were strung.

Tables covered in red-and-white checkered tablecloths polka-dotted the dining area, and a service counter ran along one end, where customers placed and picked up to-go orders or purchased merchandise from the small gift area near the doors.

I led Mary to the counter, where Mrs. Carin spoke to another customer. Her graying blond hair was pulled back in a short ponytail, and her eyes sparkled as she laughed at whatever the woman had said.

She winked when she saw us and turned our way when the customer moved on. "Louisa Eggers, how are you sweet girl?" She opened her arms and leaned across the counter to hug me. "Bless your heart. You brought eggs." She smiled at Mary. "I need those bad. My delivery man won't be here until the day after tomorrow, and I've been as nervous as a long-tailed cat in a room full of rocking chairs. Just sure I'd run out before breakfast."

"Sounds like we're just in time," I said. "This is Mary Acres. I don't think y'all have met. Mary raises Plymouth Rock hens, and I thought you might like to try some of their eggs."

Mrs. Carin extended a hand to Mary, and I waited while they talked shop a beat, negotiating price and discussing the possibility of additional orders. "I do love a free-range egg," she said.

A brunette in a logoed polo carried a wooden crate to an empty table near the window and swapped out the place setting and centerpiece while I watched. She fussed over the tablecloth, then cleaned the window before standing back to admire her work.

Mary turned to stare as well. "What's she doing?"

"Oh." Mrs. Carin leaned against the counter, trouble creasing her brow. "The man from the town website called today and set up an appointment to come by for dinner. He says he plans to review the place for the Town Yum. I'm a wreck. Lisa's just trying to make sure his table is perfect." She waved a hand to the brunette picking invisible lint from the chair.

"Dirk Yoder is coming here?" I said. "Today?" He hadn't said a word about picking up the torch so soon after Mr. Flint's death. I traded a look with Mary, wondering what she was thinking, because I had about a dozen things on my mind.

"Did he mention this?" Mary asked, turning to face me. "What's the hurry, anyway? He can't wait for the funeral before he starts posting reviews in Flint's stead?"

Mrs. Carin's gaze jumped from Mary to me. "Do you know Dirk?"

I shook my head. "Not really, but I spoke with him briefly, and he didn't say anything about this." Not that it had come up. I waved a hand, knocking my words away. "It's no big deal. I'm sure he'll be kind and fair. And everyone loves this place, so you have nothing to worry about."

Mrs. Carin didn't look convinced. "I hope so. I'm sorry Souffle the Day didn't get a better review. You didn't deserve that."

I inhaled deeply, unsure what to say.

Lisa finished fussing over the table and came to join us. "All set."

"Good. Thank you, Lisa." Mrs. Carin smiled. "This is Mary. Why don't you take her to my office and get her a check for these eggs. Then set up a tentative schedule for additional deliveries."

Mary's eyes widened at the mention of payment, and she hurried away on Lisa's heels.

"When will you reopen the café?" Mrs. Carin asked. "Soon, I hope."

"I'm not sure, but I might know more this afternoon. I'm on my way to talk to Officer Anthony now."

She straightened, as if tuning in to my terror. "I'm sure it's good news."

"Fingers crossed." My gaze wandered, unable to hold her eye contact. "Can I order a vanilla chai tea latte and a fritter to go? I probably shouldn't arrive at the police station empty-handed."

Mrs. Carin patted the counter. "Your mama clearly raised you right. I'll be back."

Hopefully I wouldn't need Mama to bail me out of jail. She told me moving away from Laurelwood would start me on a bad path, and being arrested for murder would give her the impression she'd been right.

My head lightened, and I felt the makings of a panic attack.

My life was officially out of control.

I caught the attention of a passing waiter as he dropped a pair of sunglasses into a basket marked Lost and Found. "Excuse me." My tongue swelled as the anxiety took hold. "I'm going to run to the restroom while Mrs. Carin gets my order. Will you let her know if she gets back here before I do?"

He looked me over and nodded. "Sure."

"Thank you." I hurried down the long hall toward the ladies' room. I longed to puff into a paper bag, but I'd have to settle for putting my head between my knees.

*I will not cry*, I chanted internally… *I won't freak out. Officer Anthony isn't going to arrest me, because I am innocent. I will be calm until I have good reason to be otherwise.*

I pushed into the blessedly empty restroom and selected a stall, then leaned against the closed door, willing myself to settle down. The rush of emotion had hit without warning and nearly pulled me under. I hoped my instability wouldn't increase when I arrived at the police station. Officer Anthony would think I was hiding something for sure.

*Breathe, Louisa*, I coaxed.

*Everything is fine.*

*I am fine.*

The door to the restroom creaked open and footfalls echoed off the tile floor.

I held my breath, imagining a killer on the other side.

"Louisa?" Mary called.

I exhaled long and slow. "Here. Did you get the paper-work sorted?" I asked, working to maintain a calm exterior as I opened the stall and stepped out.

"Yeah." Her eyes narrowed as she watched me. "I'm all set up to sell eggs here. Are you ready to go?"

I nodded, then moved toward the door, suddenly craving fresh air and sunshine.

Her arm bobbed up to block my path. "Wait a minute. Aren't you going to wash your hands?" The expression on her face was pure disgust, and I felt shame rising through my limbs.

"I didn't—," I started, then looked at the stall I'd exited. "I mean, I was in there, but I wasn't—"

Her brows rose, and she crossed her arms.

I sighed, then changed directions, washing my hands thoroughly and drying them with exaggerated care.

"Thank you," she said.

Mary held the door when I finished.

"I need to stop at the counter on our way out," I said, pointing to the register as Mary veered toward the front door. "I ordered coffee and a pastry for Officer Anthony."

Mary glared. "That's ridiculous."

"It's manners. Maybe she has good news."

"If she doesn't, I'm eating her pastry."

I hurried to the counter, where two members of the waitstaff wiped a spill off the floor.

Their eyes were wide when they noticed my approach.

The young woman lifted wads of soaking paper towels. "I'm so sorry," she said. "I didn't see what happened. I was with the line of customers."

The man helping her mop up the mess looked apologetically in my direction. "We were busy," he explained. "I had to seat a large group."

The familiar feeling of being watched crept along the back of my neck as I took in the complete scene before me.

A take-out cup, presumably mine, had been crushed into an accordion, splitting its side and expelling its contents over the counter and floor. A white pastry bag sat in the countertop puddle—with a knife jammed through its center.

## CHAPTER EIGHTEEN

*I* raised a hand to the Weathervane staff members attempting to clean up my latest threat. "Wait." I smiled tightly at incoming customers and forced a brief apology through trembling lips. "Pardon."

The pair who'd been attempting to erase the evidence hurried to seat and accommodate waiting patrons, while I took a cleansing breath and accessed my phone's camera. I sent photos of what was left to Officer Anthony as I took them, wishing I'd left the restroom a few moments sooner. I might've gotten a look at the culprit or even caught them in the act.

Mrs. Carin stared wide-eyed as I tucked the phone away. "What on earth!"

"May I have a couple of large freezer bags and some gloves?" I asked, lips and voice trembling, betraying my façade of calm.

A passing busboy hustled away from his place behind the counter and returned with my requests.

Mrs. Carin remained frozen. "I don't understand. What is this? Why are you taking photos of a mess in my restaurant?"

Her cheeks darkened as she took in the prying eyes of silent onlookers at nearby tables.

"Sorry," I said. "I think this is another threat meant for me. It happened while I was in the ladies' room. Normally, I'd call the police, but since I'm already on my way there, and your staff had it mostly cleaned"—and the crime scene thoroughly disturbed—"I figured I'd send photos and take the evidence with me."

I snapped on the gloves and stuffed the smashed cup, pastry bag and knife into makeshift evidence bags. I'd unfortunately seen the police do similar things enough times in the recent past to remember protocol, even if I didn't have official equipment.

Mary returned to my side, having disappeared when I'd started taking photos. "No one saw anything," she said. "It's ridiculous. There are a ton of people here, and I talked to at least a dozen. It's as if they all just wander around in little bubbles."

"Crowds are like that," I said. "Statistically, a person in need is more likely to get help if there's only a single person in the area than if there are dozens. Crowds are dangerous."

"And stupid," she groused.

I winced as a few lookie-loos frowned. "Sorry about the mess," I told Mrs. Carin. "We'll get out of your way now."

Mary leveled everyone in sight with a hard warning glare, then turned and stormed away.

I peeled off my gloves and followed.

The sun was blinding as I exited the building. I blinked rapidly to adjust my vision, and a familiar silhouette came into view.

Eli moved swiftly toward us in long, purposeful strides. "Are you both okay?" He looked from me to Mary, then back.

"What are you doing here?" I asked, fresh warmth

spreading through my chest. "We're fine, but I thought you had work today."

"I do, but Mary called," he said. "I took the ATV into town. Work can wait."

Behind him, the four-wheeler he occasionally buzzed around Meadowbrook on stood near our pickup.

Mary recapped the situation when my words failed, then outlined her general disappointment with people. Eli crossed his arms and absorbed every word.

"You should've called the police," he said.

I released a small puff of breath. "Why? To what end?" Desperation soured my stomach and rose through my chest and throat like poison. "It was half cleaned up when I found it, and Officer Anthony is probably waiting to arrest me as we speak."

Groups of people drifted from the restaurant, whispering as they crossed the lot to their vehicles. I imagined Mama's phone exploding from the number of incoming texts.

.  Eli scanned the curious faces before moving toward the truck. "Help me get the four-wheeler into the bed. I'm going with you guys."

We pulled the boards used as a ramp for loading heavy items into place, then Eli guided the small vehicle into the back of the truck and secured it.

A moment later, we were on our way.

Eli drove. Mary seemed too likely to hit a pedestrian out of spite, and I was too shaken to do more than scoot into the center of the bench seat and hold the evidence bags.

I tried to take up less space as I knocked into Eli, then Mary, as we rounded one corner, then another.

No one spoke until we reached the small Cromwell PD parking lot.

The police station was a lackluster brown-and-tan single-story building that used to be a strip mall with a bank and an insurance company. The structure had been renovated when I was in middle school, after it was purchased by the town. Now, each officer had their own office. A lady my mama went to church with answered the phones, and the reinforced walls of the former bank vaults held evidence from crimes, the force's small arsenal and two holding cells.

Eli held the door and waited while we entered.

I approached the desk with shaky limbs and fear icing me from head to toe.

Kay Abernathy took my name and made a call from the landline unit on her desk. Bright blue eye shadow climbed her lids to meet thin, penciled on eyebrows. "Officer Anthony, Ms. Eggers is here." Her gaze flicked to my entourage. "That's right." She pressed her lips together and returned the receiver to its cradle. "She's on her—"

"I didn't realize I sent out a group invitation," Officer Anthony said, appearing several feet away, outside an open office door.

Kay let her eyes fall shut, ever the nervous Nelly, and she mouthed the word *sorry* as I passed.

"Good luck," Mary stage whispered.

"We'll be right here when you finish," Eli added.

I nodded and fought the urge to demand she not repeat any of this to my mother. Or any of their congregation. Those church ladies would be live wires with news like this.

"Mary drove me to town," I told the officer, clearing my throat twice to get the words out. "Eli escorted us here after the mishap at The Weathervane."

Her lids drooped slightly in a bland, unhappy expression. "The Weathervane," she repeated, each word a low growl in her throat. "In addition to your texts, I received at least ten calls in half as many minutes on that subject." She turned and moved through the open office door at her side. "The chief headed over there to interview the workers and any guests hanging around. I'm surprised you missed him."

I followed her as far as the threshold, raising the bags in front of me. "I brought the evidence."

"Get in here." She motioned me closer with a whipping wrist. "And your entourage," she called, projecting her voice. "All of you. And close the door."

We filed into the small office and stared at the two chairs opposite Officer Anthony's desk.

Mary took one seat. Eli tipped his head, indicating I should take the other.

I accepted and set the evidence bags on the desk.

Unlike the simple, frill-less building we'd walked through, Officer Anthony's office was warm and welcoming. Plants grew in colorful pots along the windowsill, leafy and green. Photos of smiling faces and beautiful places lined her credenza, and framed degrees and specialization certifications hung on the walls. From the look of things, Officer Anthony had a nice little life outside the uniform, complete with two curly haired dogs, many friends and a zest for travel. She'd studied law enforcement at a college in Texas and served in the US Airforce.

I felt my brows rising and lips pulling down as my brain grunted, *huh.*

A half heartbeat later, I realized I was more like my mother than I'd realized. I'd unfairly drawn conclusions about Officer Anthony based on her starchy uniform, serious demeanor and painfully sleek low bun. If anyone had asked two minutes ago, I'd have imagined her a friendless, joyless grouch and probably a control freak. The contents of her office painted a new picture entirely.

"Ms. Eggers?" she asked, pulling my eyes to hers.

I blinked as the new, fuller image of her fell into place. "Hmm? Sorry."

Her jaw tightened and she took a breath, presumably for patience. "You say you don't know why Mr. Flint arrived at your souffle shop on the night of his death, yet his phone shows you texted him and asked him to come. Care to explain that?"

"What?" I frowned. "I didn't text Mr. Flint that day. I was in town when he arrived."

I told her about my run-in with my mother and Mrs. Carin. The time I'd spent at Corner Cup and speaking to the receptionist outside the newspaper. "Mary ran the café for me, because I wasn't even there."

Officer Anthony opened a manila folder and slid the top sheet of paper in my direction. "Not being there when he arrived doesn't mean you didn't send the messages."

I wondered if the same logic applied to Dirk Yoder.

Mary craned her neck for a look at the paper, printed with a series of text exchanges. "We need to talk about your awful article! Please come over right away, or I will get my attorney involved for slander," she read. Her green eyes flicked to mine and she snorted. "This person cannot spell awful. It doesn't need two Ls. Come on. And Louisa would never write any of that," she told the officer. "Whoever is responsible for this nonsense obviously doesn't know her at all. She would've approached this guy gently and killed him with kindness."

The room stilled, and Mary's bemused expression flattened.

"Poor word choice," she said. "You know what I mean. Louisa's a marshmallow."

I offered my friend a small pressed-lips smile. She and I hadn't gotten off on the right foot initially, but seeing this woman, who kind of hated everyone, stand up for me sent a bolt of confidence through my heart. "She's right," I said. "I do my best not to step on toes or escalate already-tense situations. I was taught to catch flies with honey."

"Now, her mother, on the other hand," Mary said. "She's the Eggers who'd hire an attorney."

"Correct." My mother's voice cracked through the room.

I turned to the open doorway, where Mama stood beside Eli, who'd apparently let her in.

A small man with a tan suit, bad comb-over, and briefcase moved into view.

"Officer Anthony," Mama said. "This is my attorney, Herman Cross. You can direct your questions to him now. My daughter is finished talking."

"Mama," I said. "What are you doing here?"

"A very wise friend called me." She lifted her chin, shoulders square and looking powerful in her smart navy dress. A designer bag hung from the crook of one arm.

I turned wide eyes on Mary. First she'd called Eli. Now Mama? "Is there anyone you didn't call while I cleaned up that mess?"

Mary wrinkled her nose. "I didn't call her. She's my new boss. You think I want her associating me with this trainwreck?"

"Then—" I swiveled on my seat again, eyes flashing to Eli. "You?"

He dipped his chin in one stiff nod, expression unapologetic. "I know this routine," he said. "I spent three days here when I was a suspect. You shouldn't have to."

My jaw dropped, and I longed to tell him exactly what I thought about him making decisions for me. I knew Mama's number. I could've called her anytime I wanted. I hadn't because I didn't want her involved.

I spun back to face Officer Anthony, hands folded neatly in my lap and a pleasant expression on my face, while I seethed inside.

Mr. Cross handled the rest of the officer's questions and left his business card before escorting me back to the parking lot several minutes later. A black town car waited for him and Mama.

She looked at the work truck we'd arrived in, a muddy four-wheeler secured in the bed, then sighed. "Why don't you come home and spend a few days with me while this is all sorted? You can bring Thelma. Bring all the animals if you want. There's plenty of room. I can send someone to transport them."

"No, Mama," I said, planting a kiss on her cheek. "I'm okay. Thank you for coming." I looked to Mr. Cross, then back to Mama, extending the appreciation to them both.

Mr. Cross climbed into the town car, while Mama hugged me tight.

She extended a hand to Eli. "Thank you," she said, eyes traveling the full length of him in a slick appraisal. "How well do you like your current work situation, Mr. Fogle?"

He frowned.

"Don't answer that," I said.

He looked to me, then back to Mama without speaking.

Mama sighed. "Very well. My offer stands, and you know how to reach me."

He nodded in acceptance.

Mama's expression grew bored and disappointed. She turned her eyes back to me. "Please be safe and know I'd gladly make this trip a thousand times rather than see you at a hospital even once. You are my heart, and I must insist you be careful."

"I won't need a hospital," I promised.

She sniffed, then joined Mr. Cross in the car, and it rolled away.

## CHAPTER NINETEEN

*M*ary, Eli and I packed into the truck again and headed home.

Eli drove.

Mary leaned around me in the cab, speaking directly to him, as if I were a sack of potatoes inconveniently in her way. "You called her mother? Are you crazy?"

"Yes," Eli said. "And no, I'm not crazy. I'd gladly do it again."

Mary huffed and faced forward once more. "Now I look like trouble, being involved in this today, and she just hired me."

My mind raced with a thousand things I wanted to voice but needed to process. I started with the one bothering me most. "Officer Anthony said the lab confirmed it was soy in my cream bottle. How is that possible?"

"Someone switched it," Mary said. "Obviously."

"Okay, but who? Who has access to the refrigerator at Souffle the Day? Other than us?"

Mary looked at me without answering.

Eli slowed at the traffic light and offered, "Maybe the

exchange happened before the container got to you. Who delivered it?"

I tried to remember. Sometimes the neighbors brought my orders to me. Sometimes I stopped by and picked them up. And on occasion, when they were especially busy... "The milk truck."

On weeks Mr. Thompson had a large number of orders, a milk truck from the Cromwell dairy picked them up and delivered them with their own. Mr. Thompson had compared it to ordering a single Uber for three dozen dairy shipments.

"Great," Mary said. "We can find out who the driver was and talk to him."

Eli drummed his thumbs on the steering wheel. "I'll talk to Mr. Thompson."

"Wait a minute," I said, a memory slamming into mind. "I think someone was in my shop the night before Mr. Flint died." I turned to Mary. "Do you remember being in my backyard, upset about the article, and telling me I'd left a light on in the shop?"

I felt Eli turn to face me, and Mary's gaze on my opposite cheek.

I stared into the distance, trying to recall the details of the night. "I assumed I'd forgotten to turn the light off, until I got there and saw the utility door against the back wall was unlocked. I never unlock it, because I never use it. Nothing was damaged or missing, so I had no reason to assume an unlocked door was a sign of nefarious doings. But what if someone unlocked the door so they could come back after I closed and switch the cream for soy, then sent the bogus texts the next day, encouraging Mr. Flint to return?"

"I don't know about the details," Mary said, "but that's premeditation."

"More like assassination," Eli said.

"If someone was conniving enough to do all that," Mary said, "why leave the light on when they left? Why not cover their tracks?"

My stomach coiled and ached as the night flashed through my mind with new clarity. "I'd felt watched," I whispered.

The words were barely audible in the small cab, and realization struck anew. "I think I interrupted a killer."


Eli stuck by my side all afternoon and evening. He'd asked for help with a few of his chores, then followed me back to my place to finish mine. When we'd run out of things to do, he started on the new pasture fence I'd purchased for Jack and Jill.

Memories of Eli with a post-hole digger were my new happy place.

His shirt clung to the planes and angles of his broad chest as he drank from a jug of spring water he'd hauled over from his place. Apparently glasses were impractical for a lumberjack. They spilled and broke too easily. A jug, however, was just what he needed. He'd guzzled nearly half the water already, and soon the other half would be gone.

I tried not to stare each time he crooked an arm to heft the container, tightening his short sleeve around his biceps.

I didn't track the little beads of sweat on his handsome face or tanned neck. Didn't peek at the band of exposed skin above his jeans each time he raised both hands to adjust his hat or run a hand through sweaty hair.

And I definitely didn't fantasize about spraying him off with my garden hose or suggesting we cool off together with a swim in the nearby creek.

Mostly because if I saw the man in nothing but swim trunks, my young life might be cut abruptly short.

"I like it," he said, his low rumbling voice causing me to flinch.

If he'd somehow seen into my head, I was in trouble.

I followed his gaze to the completed fencing outside Jack and Jill's small barn. I'd arranged small wooden bridges and platforms throughout the grass as enrichment, landing spots and obstacles for them to walk over and around. Afterward, I'd hung baskets filled with donkey-friendly branches from the overhang of their shelter's roof so they could munch on a variety of greens at will. And with every last ounce of my stamina, I'd created a play pond by digging a perfectly measured hole and sinking a plastic kiddie pool in it. I'd tossed apples and ice cubes into the water for their entertainment.

"Where do you get all these ideas?" Eli asked, smiling at the happy couple.

"Mama," I said. "Tough as she is on humans, she's a devoted animal lover. I grew up following her around the Laurelwood property and living museum, checking on produce, workers and animals. She took special care to see that the livestock were happy and fulfilled. Never bored, sad or lonely."

He set the water jug aside with fresh tension in his eyes. "Are you mad I called her today?"

"No. Not anymore. You were right to do it, and I probably should've done it myself."

Thelma and several of the other hens ducked under the bottom rung of the new fence, approaching Jack and Jill's little pool with cocked heads and enthusiastic clucks.

I sighed. I hadn't spent enough time with her the last couple of days, and it was nice to see her happy.

"I was thinking," Eli said. "Not to get you going again about Flint's death, but I don't suppose you still have that nanny cam for your chickens? Maybe it caught a look at whoever snuck into your shop."

"Nope." I'd let my monthly subscription to a live feed on my hens run out when I was setting a budget for my café. All extra cash was redirected to the start-up.

I crossed my arms as a wave of insecurity crashed through me. "I'm sure I cooked with cream all that morning, but there was a second container available. I keep a backup of everything in case I run out. I didn't have any reason to touch it."

"What happened to the second container?" he asked.

I looked to the distant souffle stand. "I don't know. I guess it's probably still in there, unless it was the one Officer Anthony took." I hadn't been inside the café since she'd left with the soy in a bag. I felt the familiar pangs of frustration tightening my throat and core. "I can't stand this. The case against me just keeps getting tighter. If I'm put in jail, who will take care of Thelma and the other hens? Jack and Jill too? I've already had to find someone else to buy Mary's eggs. I'm letting everyone down, and I hate it."

Eli moved to my side. "You're not going to jail, because you're not a killer. You're a scapegoat."

I huffed a tiny laugh. "You have too much faith in the system."

His expression darkened, then cleared, as if I'd somehow hit a nerve. He looked away, apparently not planning to share his thoughts.

"I can't get past Flint's wife lying about being here," I said, steering the conversation away from whatever had upset him. "Why would she do that unless she was the one who replaced my cream? She could've come back to make sure her plan to get rid of him worked. Or she could've somehow administered the soy herself."

"Was she also here the day before?" Eli asked. "Could she have unlocked the utility door for a later return?"

"Maybe." I chewed my lip, thinking back to the day before my current nightmare began. "I wish I remembered seeing her. At least then I could take this theory to the police. But I'm not sure I did. She felt completely unfamiliar when I met her at Pop Off."

He folded his arms and considered me. "She could've asked someone to unlock the door for her."

That was true enough, and an innocuous request. "How can I find out if anyone was asked to do that?" I wondered aloud. "Do you think I could persuade Wilhelmina to post the question in the paper?"

He tipped his head. "If you do that, you should definitely plan on staying at your mom's afterward, because if you're right, the killer will be looking to stop you from meeting whoever did their initial dirty work."

I grimaced. "That would just cause a killer to turn up on my mama's doorstep. That doesn't seem right of me."

"You're welcome to stay at my place," Eli said.

I opened my mouth, then shut it, torn between telling him that was too much to ask and running to pack my bags. "I don't know. I don't want to endanger you either. Though, you're probably in better shape to fight off a killer than my mother and her staff."

"Probably," he said, lips twitching in amusement.

I wondered about the truth behind that single word. Who had Eli been before Meadowbrook?

"Your mom misses you," he said.

"I miss her too."

He squinted against the waning sun. "It was nice of you to let her help today."

"I didn't have a lot of choice when she showed up with her lawyer," I said, enunciating the final three words.

Eli laughed, and I joined him.

"Was she at least nice when you called her?"

He nodded. "Very. She was surprised, then a little panicked. I think she'd move mountains to spare you a moment of unhappiness. You're a lucky woman to be loved like that."

I bit my lip, knowing he was right and wondering what made him so interested in my relationship with Mama. "How were you able to reach her?" Surely Mama's number wasn't a matter of public knowledge.

"I called the living museum. The woman who answered put me on hold and went to get her."

"Oh." I bobbed my head. That was a completely reasonable explanation. I wasn't sure what I thought he might say. Though something else wiggled in the back of my mind, sliding just out of reach when I tried to grasp it.

I moved to my patio table and sat.

Eli joined me. "You might want to consider staying with me until this is over," he said again. "Or I can stay here, if you'd prefer, but I've got a gut feeling things are coming to a head. The threats are escalating, coming closer and more boldly. I don't want you to be alone when the killer cracks."

"You could stay here," I said, tracking Thelma's path around the donkey pool. "If you think that's best. But I don't want to leave the animals."

"Well, then," he said. "It's a plan."

The memory I'd been chasing snapped back like a rubber band, and I swiveled on my chair to face him. "Hey. Before Mama left us at the police station, she said something to you."

Eli stiffened, and I suspected he knew what I was about to say. "What?"

"She said her offer stood. What offer? What did she mean?"

He looked away momentarily, before returning the full weight of his hazel gaze to me. "She offered me a position as head of security at Laurelwood."

I gaped. "Why would she do that?"

"She said you trust me, so she trusts me."

"But why does Mama need a head of security? It's not as if she has a security team. And why does she think you're the man for the job?" I recalled Mama's presumption that Eli was former military and wondered if she'd looked into that or if it was truly a guess. "Is something going on over there?"

Then something new occurred, and my eyes narrowed. "Does she think I'll go home if you live at Laurelwood?"

Eli's frown vanished and a smile bloomed. "Why would she think that?"

The size of my massive misstep registered, and I made an inarticulate noise. "I don't know," I said finally. "She's just always plotting to get me to go back."

Eli watched me squirm, amusement dancing in his eyes.

"Wait," I said, a nearly forgotten conversation returning to mind. "When I spoke with Jeanie at The Pretty Pantry a few days ago she said Mama thought someone was stealing from her at Laurelwood. I hadn't given it much thought at the time, because Mama is a force of nature, and my mind was already on this thing with Mr. Flint. But what if she's worried?"

"I think you should ask her about it."

I dragged my gaze to Jack and Jill as they grazed, refusing to meet Eli's eye while I processed. If Mama needed help, he should help. And so should I.

Eli's phone dinged with a text message, and he removed it from his pocket to take a look.

My mind jumped back to our time at the police station. "Officer Anthony said I could've sent those bogus texts, pretending to be home, even if I wasn't. It was just like our talk with Dirk Yoder. He made a point of telling us he couldn't be the killer, because I was threatened at his house, but he wasn't there. Are Dirk and I in the same boat? Or is this all by his design? Planned misdirects and chaos?"

"I've wondered the same thing," Eli said, tucking his phone back into his pocket. "I've been thinking about the printed messages Officer Anthony showed us. The author misspelled awful. It's a pretty common word. Maybe the author was in a hurry."

"The article that started all this was terribly written too. Coincidence?"

Eli's brows raised. "Unlikely."

"It wouldn't make any sense for the killer to slander me with that review before killing the man who supposedly wrote it. Right? If they wanted him dead, why not focus on that?"

Eli's jaw locked and his gaze hardened. "What if this was never about Flint? What if it's always been about you?"

## CHAPTER TWENTY

*a*fter a long, sleepless night with Eli on my couch and Thelma on her roost in my sunroom, I decided to visit Mama. I wore a dress she'd bought me while I still lived at home and asked Eli to drop me off at Laurelwood after breakfast.

Mama met me at the door with open arms. Her gray dress slacks and sleeveless peach silk blouse enhanced her youthful figure and dewy complexion. Her fawn peep-toe pumps matched her understated, but meticulously applied, lipstick and eyeshadow. Mama was nearly twenty years older than me, but there were days we looked more like sisters. Today was one of them. "There's my baby girl," she said, ushering me inside. "I have coffee and muffins in the kitchen. There's also fresh fruit and a kettle for tea."

I followed the heavenly aromas to Mama's enormous chef's kitchen. She prided herself on keeping Laurelwood's decor authentic and true to the era in which it was built, but the kitchen was her domain. As a result, the space had received its second makeover in my lifetime last summer.

Mama didn't mess around when it came to food, and she believed her ancestors would wholly understand.

The massive white granite island at the room's center was loaded with fruits, muffins, gourmet breakfast breads and spreads.

I helped myself to a croissant and added a dollop of strawberry preserves while Mama poured me a mug of coffee. I sliced a banana as well and shook cinnamon on the pieces.

Mama carried my drink to the little table set before an expanse of floor-to-ceiling windows overlooking the rear garden. "I'm so glad you came," she said. "I have something special planned today, and I know you're going to like it. So, after you eat, why don't you run upstairs and change? Then we'll get started."

I looked at my dress, then at Mama. "You bought me this outfit. You don't like it anymore?" I set my plate beside the steaming coffee mug, then took the chair across from hers.

"I bought that for you while you were in college. You're not some carefree coed anymore, darling. You're an adult. You should dress like one."

I stuffed a muffin into my mouth before I complained. Mama always made me older than I was, insisting on another level of intensity, growth or maturity. Whether I was ready or not. I'd heard similar sentiments from her a dozen times. "Louisa, you aren't a baby anymore. You're in first grade now. Act like it. Louisa, you're a high schooler. Louisa, you're in college."

*Act like it.*

I let my eyelids fall shut, then pried them open, knowing Mama had raised me the same way she'd been raised, with an abundance of love, twice as many rules and even more expectations.

"What?" She lifted her teacup for a sip. "You'll be twenty-seven soon. That's a lot closer to thirty than twenty."

I took a deep breath. "I'm still a young woman, Mama. I'm unburdened and happy." All thoughts of a killer trying to murder me aside. "I hope that will continue no matter how old I get. And I like this dress."

"You operate your own business. You own a home and property and raise blue-ribbon hens. I don't know what else you need to realize you're grown." She took another demure sip, then added, "Maybe a husband would help."

My eyelids drooped, and suspicion kicked in. Had I been bamboozled? "What exactly do you have planned for me, Mama? You aren't trying to set me up are you? Because I'm not looking for a husband. I don't want to date. I'm happy just as I am."

She made a show of rolling her eyes, slow and exaggerated. "No one is happy alone, dear. Don't be foolish."

"I'm serious. I happen to make excellent company, and I enjoy myself fully."

She leveled me with her most superior stare. "What do you do when you can't reach something on a shelf?"

"I have a stepladder."

"What if you need to open a jar?"

"I tap the lid. I use a gripper. I knock it gently against the counter." I would cheerfully smash the thing in my sink and clean up the pieces before I'd marry a man on the off chance I might, one day, have a jar-opening emergency.

Mama sighed. "I'm not trying to fix you up. That's not the surprise. But we can talk about that another day. Now, finish your muffin and go change."

I'd lost my appetite, which worked in Mama's favor since she was in such a hurry to get me moving.

I dragged myself up the stairs and found two dresses laid out on my old bed. One blue. One red. Both identical otherwise. Short sleeves, scoop neckline, fitted waist, and a bell-shaped skirt.

I chose red and slid bare feet into the white sandals waiting between the dresses.

The front doorbell rang before I made it down the steps to the foyer.

Constance answered, and Tina Flint walked inside.

She wore a black one-piece jumper that billowed at the legs when she walked. The cap sleeves fluttered in the wind from the closing door. Her floppy hat and sunglasses completed the ensemble.

My gaze jerked around the room, as I stood frozen on the stairs. What on earth was Tina Flint doing at Laurelwood? She was clearly in mourning. And as far as I knew, not a friend of Mama's.

The familiar click of heels over marble drew my attention to Mama as she approached. She opened her arms, greeting Tina with cheek kisses, before inviting her into the parlor.

I trailed them with my eyes.

Mama glared, and motioned one hand against the underside of her chin, warning me to shut my gaping mouth.

I hurried down the steps to meet them.

"Thank you for coming." Mama spoke again as I entered the dramatic cream-and-rose-colored room.

The room was full of light and reeked of femininity with its floral wallpaper and tufted velvet chairs. White woodwork outlined a row of neatly spaced windows overlooking the side yard and a bay window facing the fountain out front.

I lowered onto a cream settee, while Mama and Tina took the sage-green armchairs near a small tea cart and coffee table.

"Thank you for having me," Tina said. "I have to admit I was a little surprised by the invitation."

"Oh," Mama said sweetly. "I try to entertain every shop

owner at some time. It's good to know who's who in the community. It makes it easier for me to support them properly when needed. It's so important to stand by our small businesses. Don't you agree, Louisa?"

I blinked when I realized both ladies had turned to me. "Yes," I croaked. "Absolutely."

"And women supporting women is doubly grand," Mama said.

Tina nodded, seeming confused but willing to roll with it.

Mama pointed a finger where it rested on her lap, covertly indicating the bright-pink purse I'd asked about on my last visit. She raised one eyebrow in prompt.

When I opened and closed my mouth without words, she took the lead once more.

"What a lovely handbag," Mama said. "Where did you find something so unusual? I'm a bit of a connoisseur myself."

Tina squirmed. "Thank you. It's an Sophia Cardiff."

"Oh?" Mama clasped her hands. "I love Sophia's work. She's a dear friend of mine. I've spent more money in her store than I have on some of the cars I've purchased."

Mama laughed, but Tina's gaze traveled back to me.

I took that as my cue. "You know, I ran into Sophia just the other day," I said, crossing my ankles and widening my eyes in that innocent southern lady way Mama had taught me. I set my palms in my lap and filled my voice with faux innocence and enthusiasm. "She sends her regards, Mama."

"Isn't she the sweetest?"

I swept my gaze and cherubic expression back to Tina. "Turns out nothing's changed in her policies, and she still only makes each design once. She even has a three-ring binder with photos of every bag. I had a look at them."

"Really?" Mama asked. "How delightful. I'll bet I've got my own binder over there. Did you happen to see Mrs. Flint's bag?"

Mrs. Flint stilled, and her eyes locked with mine.

"I did. I also saw that bag at my souffle stand on the night your husband died, Mrs. Flint."

She jolted upright, eyes frantically searching the room.

The only way out was the way she'd come, and that meant passing both Mama and me.

"I know you were there," I said, rising as well. "What I don't know is why you'd lie about it."

Unless she'd been there to kill him or watch him die.

Her chin wobbled, and her face twisted into a knot. Then the tears began to fall.

Mama reached lazily for the box of tissues on the coffee table and extended them in our guest's direction.

Mrs. Flint pulled several from the box and retook her seat, dabbing at her eyes. "I was following him. To see if he was with another woman."

I cocked my head, unsure if this was a ruse. I'd seen her temper before. Sudden tears were unexpected. "Why would you think that?"

"I don't know. Because I left him, I guess. I left, and he didn't chase me." She sucked in a gasping breath, then sobbed. "He was supposed to chase me."

Mama pulled her chin back and cocked a brow, visibly horrified by the woman's outburst. Mama would sooner walk to town in cutoff jean shorts than behave like Tina in front of virtual strangers.

"He was spending so much time with you," she said between racking sobs, causing Mama's face to contort, as if she smelled something bad. "I hated it."

I groaned. "I've already told you that wasn't the case." The man was far too old, and obviously liked fashionable, age-appropriate women, like his wife. "Look at you. You're gorgeous, and he married you. What on earth would he want with me?"

Tina gave a low, humorless laugh. "Oh, you know what."

Mama smacked her palms on the arms of her chair. "Do not say it," Mama warned. "Do not insult my daughter, or you will be quite sorry."

I bit my lip, torn between wanting to defend myself and wanting to see Mama lose her unyielding control.

"He'd already finished his article on your café," Tina said. "Why else would he go back if not to see you for... scandalous reasons?"

"Because he's twice my age," I squawked. "And married!"

"Someone texted him, claiming to be Louisa," Mama provided, redirecting our exchange. "The poser demanded to talk about his article on Souffle the Day. It was a trick."

Tina's brow furrowed, and she pressed the tissues to each cheek slowly. "What?"

"It wasn't me. The police showed us the messages."

Her arms fell limply at her sides. "Someone lured him there?"

"It appears that way," I said, struggling to make the pieces of the puzzle fit.

Her confusion became palpable, and I knew Tina wasn't the culprit. She was stunned, horrified and grieving, but not a killer.

My heart softened. "Mrs. Flint, I assure you there wasn't anything untoward happening between me and your husband. We talked about Meadowbrook and the souffle stand. Nothing else. He seemed truly interested in my community and gave every impression he planned to promote Souffle the Day with his write-up. I was genuinely gobsmacked when I read his review."

Her eyes unfocused, as if something had broken her concentration. "It was odd. The article, I mean. And the writing was atrocious. Not like him at all. He was such a stickler for details. I thought maybe he was so heartbroken and miserable after I left that he'd stopped trying or caring." She sniffed, and the tears began to fall again.

Mama called Constance to bring a pot of tea.

My gaze fell on a familiar pickup rolling into the driveway outside the bay window. "Excuse me," I said, rising to meet my friend.

I slid onto the porch with a smile.

Mary climbed down from the truck looking angry as usual. "Can this place be any bigger?" she complained. "Seriously. I'm asking. It's like you grew up in a kingdom."

"It's nice to see you too." I gave the truck another look, then scanned the land around us for signs of Eli, who was supposed to take me home.

"Eli's coming on the four-wheeler," she said. "He insisted I take the truck because I'm a woman and he's a misogynist. He had a stop to make first, and has to take trails or some other nonsense because the ATV isn't road legal. He'll be here as soon as he can."

I tried not to get too excited about the concept of riding Eli's four-wheeler with him.

"I'm here for an orientation. Where am I supposed to go?" Mary asked. "Where do I park? I can't just leave this thing here, and I was told not to park in the visitor lot."

I gave the house a long look, hoping Mama wouldn't be too angry if I was gone fifteen minutes instead of five, then I ran around to the passenger door. "There's hidden parking for the museum staff at the end of this driveway and on your right. Come on. I'll show you."

I moved a basket of eggs she'd belted in place, then put them on my lap. "Are these for The Weathervane?"

"No. I was already there. Which way?"

I pointed to a dirt access road at the far end of the driveway, near the place she'd turned off the main street. "There, on the right."

Mary shifted into gear and headed for the lot where living-history museum workers parked their modern-day vehicles out of sight. "I delivered a basket to Mrs. Carin on my way here," she said, picking up the conversation where we'd left off. "This basket is for someone named Julia."

"That's Mama's cook. I can take the eggs back with me."

Mary shook her head at the words "Mama's cook."

We rode in silence over the quarter mile of winding tree-lined gravel, then rocked to a stop in a field with other trucks. Employees used the path daily during the season, arriving in costume and on site with no obvious entrance or tie to modern times, as far as guests could tell.

I smiled at the carefully constructed village, partially visible through a thin line of trees. "Welcome to history."

Tinny music and distant laughter rose to our ears as we exited the vehicle. Dozens of men and women in period clothing moved over the land, working at various tasks, while volunteering children played stick ball and other games of the times. Everything smelled of warm bread and stewing meats.

Mary grimaced. "What have I agreed to?"

A woman in a plain dress, apron and bonnet appeared at the tree line's edge, one hand waving over her head. "There you are!" she called. "I'm Annalise. You're Mary? Hello, Louisa."

I waved back, recalling her name and voice more than her face. "Hello. Yes, she's Mary. She's great with animals and children," I called, earning a clap of delight from the other woman.

Mary pinched me, and I slapped her hand away.

"Come on," Annalise called. "Let's get you into costume. The morning showcase is about to begin, and we still need a stablehand and two butter churners. We should hurry."

Twice a day, performers encouraged guests to gather on

the far end of the property, where actors performed skits from various eras in Cromwell, demonstrating with music, food and humor the ways life had progressed throughout the generations. The shows were always huge hits. And the gathering of guests gave other museum workers a small reprieve from their time in character, as well as an opportunity to sit or get out of the sun.

Mary turned to me for help, and I ran away.

"Have fun at work," I called, grabbing the eggs from the front seat of the truck. "I can't wait to hear all about it."

"Oh, you're going to hear all about it," she threatened as Annalise pulled her away by one elbow.

Back on the dirt road leading to Mama's driveway, I swung the basket and tipped my chin to the sky. Anytime now, I would be on the back of Eli's four-wheeler, arms wrapped around him tight.

I listened intently for sounds of an engine, but there was nothing but noise from the museum to hear. I reached into my pocket for my phone, deciding to give Mama a heads-up. I would be back in ten minutes, and Eli would be there at any time.

A familiar figure stepped free from the shadows along the trees and raised a small handgun in my direction.

"Mrs. Carin!"

# CHAPTER TWENTY-ONE

*M*rs. Carin wore black capri pants and sneakers with a black t-shirt and matching ball cap pulled low on her forehead. Not exactly her usual attire. She waved me toward the trees, anxious eyes darting. "Come here," she demanded.

"Mrs. Carin," I said, following her gaze and scrambling mentally for a way out of whatever was happening. My heart sprinted, and my mind raced. "What's going on? Why are you here? In the trees like that?"

The hand holding her gun trembled so severely, I feared she'd shoot me without intent.

"Just—just do as I say!"

I raised my palms, Mary's egg basket hanging from the crook of one arm. "Okay. But I'm trying to understand what's happened. Why do you have that gun?"

In the distance, a round of applause went up, and I realized the living museum's morning showcase was underway. Mary, Annalise and the vast majority of other museum workers and guests were gathered on the opposite side of the property by now.

I bit my lip against the urge to scream for help, fearing the gun in her hand was meant for me, and one wrong move on my part could be my last. "Are you okay?"

"No! I am not okay!" she screeched. "And you are the reason!"

I pressed a palm to my collarbone, my mental wheels slowly beginning to turn again. "I'm so sorry. How can I fix it?"

She growled, long and slow, the vibration melding into a humorless laugh. "I think you've done enough."

I blinked as the truth of things hit like a stone.

Eli had been right last night, when he'd hypothesized the real problem. Everyone had been looking at Mr. Flint's death as if it was about him, when it had always been about me.

And my souffle stand.

Then the memories came, popping into existence one by one until my head was full and dizzy.

I'd caught Mrs. Carin hiding alongside Corner Cup, pretending to take a break from her busy café after the terrible review had increased her business and sent me on a fact-finding mission. That was probably the first day she'd followed me.

"Give me your phone," she said as I inched closer, biding my time and in no hurry to accommodate the woman planning to kill me.

"I don't understand," I said, continuing my thin ruse. "Should I call the police? Are you in danger?"

Her expression turned droll, and her free hand shot forward, fingers opening and closing in the universal sign for gimmee. "You are the one in danger, Louisa Eggers. Now, hurry up!"

I tightened my hold on the device, then froze at the sound of tires on gravel.

We turned our heads as Tina Flint's car rolled slowly

down the driveway thirty-feet away, then onto the main road without so much as a glance in our direction.

My heart sank at the loss of a potential witness, then raced with the realization Mama would be looking for me soon.

My phone dinged, and I turned my eyes to the screen.

As if on cue, it was Mama.

Mama: Where are you? Tina's gone, and I have news about that woman from The Weathervane.

"Oh, for goodness sakes," Mrs. Carin snapped. She strode forward and snatched the phone before I could respond to her or Mama. "Give me that." Her eyes widened and her cheeks flushed red as she read the words on my screen. "Darn it! Darn! Darn! Darn it!"

I scanned the ground for a limb or other makeshift weapon to defend myself, but there was only endless grass and gravel.

"That Tina Flint's got a big mouth," Mrs. Carin seethed. "I knew the minute she came into my shop complaining about you and your investigation she'd cause me trouble." She worked her thumb over the screen of my phone with more than a little effort, gaze jumping repeatedly to me, as if I might make a run for it. "Do not move," she warned. "I don't want to shoot you. I just need time to think and tell your mama that you decided to head home."

Naïve amounts of hope rose in my heart with her words. "Thank you," I said. "Not shooting me is wise. I know we can work this out, and I promise I won't tell anyone."

Her brows pinched, and she motioned again for me to move with her into the trees. "Hurry!"

"Okay. Sorry." I obeyed, entering the shadows, but staying out of arm's reach. "Let's talk it out," I suggested.

Her expression twisted. "I didn't come here to talk, you twit. I'm here to kill you. I just can't shoot you, because I know all about ballistics. I watch T.V. You're going to have an accident or take a tremendous fall. You don't have any allergies do you?"

I scoffed.

"Don't do that," she said smartly. "Don't pretend this isn't your fault. I have to do something before your ridiculous interference lands me in jail. Where would I be then?"

*In jail*, I thought, biting back my inner Mary.

"The Weathervane would fail without me, and that place was my daddy's dream, rest his soul. So, I can't stop now," she complained. "Then all of this will have been for nothing."

She waved the gun around, and I wondered how dedicated she was to *not* shooting me.

"Do you know how much time this has taken me?" she asked. "Sending you messages to leave this alone, trying not to get caught in the process. Following you and your leads, guessing who you'd contact next, then finding ways to bump into them? Using other people's phones without their notice isn't easy, and it takes a long time before they let their guards down. Buying endless burner phones isn't financially feasible, and there's always the chance of someone remembering you recently bought one. Online delivery takes at least two days. Nothing about this has been simple. It's all a colossal time suck, and I'm trying to run a business!"

Another thought came to mind. She knew all about the texting app used by the town and how to send the messages. "You sent everyone to Souffle the Day on the night Mr. Flint died," I said, slowly fitting the pieces together.

"It really is a useful tool," she said flatly. "I heard Flint complaining about how poorly it was designed by Yoder, and how anyone could send messages if they set up an account. He said it wouldn't be long before people realized and started spamming the town with gossip or junk. He was going to get the features and access locked down, but I got to it first."

I released a breath. Devious. And her café served an entire line of non-dairy products, and I was willing to bet she used soy in all of them.

My hands balled into fists at my sides, anger edging out anxiety. "You stole Dirk Yoder's phone and used it to send me those messages? Then you set up the booby trap?"

"And you still didn't give up. Getting my hands on his phone was complicated. He kept a closer eye than Flint."

I blinked. "You stole his phone too?" When? And why?

The expression of anxious determination on Mrs. Carin's face eased by a fraction, and a bit of smugness took its place. "I took it while he was chatting with a group at The Weather-vane. He checked a message, then set it on the table and turned his back as I was walking by. I couldn't resist the opportunity of a lifetime."

I bit my lip against the urge to ask how long his lifetime lasted after her stunt, and another piece of the puzzle snapped into place. "You used Mr. Flint's phone to post that review about Souffle the Day."

Her eyes danced with mischief. "He never had a clue. I took it to the ladies' room and accessed the Town Yum. His credentials were already saved. It was almost too easy. I typed a fast and terrible review, then headed out to return the phone. He was looking for it when I saw him, so I pretended to find it and asked if it was his. He was so grateful."

*Devious.*

I ground my teeth. She'd started all this. And for what? More customers? "What will you do when the crime lab confirms the soy milk taken from my fridge matches the variety you use at your café? The syrup too."

Her gaze narrowed and her jaw set. "There won't be a reason for them to check, and even if they did, it's not as if I buy a special blend. Plenty of people use the same soy and syrup."

"Do all those people have a café that stood to benefit from the elimination of Souffle the Day?"

Her cheeks darkened, and I took a tiny step back, willing my mouth to stop talking.

My phone dinged in her hand, and she looked away once more.

I scanned the trees and gravel access road, wondering if I could make a successful run for it. Her shaky hand had steadied after I moved into the trees with her, and I wasn't sure if she was a decent shot. Though even an accidental hit could kill me.

Mrs. Carin gasped, and her attention whipped back to me. "Your mother called the cops about whatever nonsense Tina said to her. That's our cue to get moving."

The phone dinged again, and she yipped. "For goodness sakes," she complained. "Now, Eli is with her. Let's go. I parked right over there."

I moved like molasses through the trees to a grassy patch off the access road, where the forest angled away.

Mrs. Carin's old Buick was wedged into the shadows, barely out of sight.

It hadn't been there when I rode past with Mary.

"Get in," she said. "Drive. I have to play coverup." She threw her car keys at me, and they bounced off my chest.

I stooped immediately to pick them up, then moved to the other side of the car, eager to add space between us. "I can't drive your car."

"Yes, you can. Now, get in or I'll shoot you." She raised the gun over the roof and I flinched as the snub barrel came to eye level.

I dumped the basket of eggs in the grass as I opened the driver's side door, hoping someone would see it and know I'd been taken.

Mrs. Carin cussed my phone, apparently still reading and responding to my mother's texts.

I climbed behind the wheel and gunned the engine to life. It'd been eight years since I'd failed the driving test five times in as many weeks, then tucked my tail and quit. I assumed my skills hadn't improved.

Everything about the moment was intense and horrible. I needed help, but I was on my own. I closed my eyes and wondered, *What would Mary do?*

Certainly *not* drive herself, and her assailant, somewhere more convenient for her murder.

Mrs. Carin wrenched open the passenger door and glaring at me across the seats without getting in. Her gaze jerked back to my phone. "Your mother is a pill. No wonder you're such a pain in my—"

I stamped on the gas and peeled away before she could finish. The Buick rocked gently over something I suspected was her foot when she wailed in pain.

A gunshot cracked through the air as I turned onto Mama's long driveway. The rear windshield shattered. Glass fragments rained down. Some exploded inward. The bullet lodged in the glass above the dashboard, creating an instant spiderweb across my line of sight.

The scream that ripped out of me was horror-film worthy. I banged my palms against the wheel, sounding the horn in rapid succession, desperate to gain attention.

A second shot followed, and the steering wheel jerked beneath my palms, setting me on a new trajectory across the grass.

I wrestled the car back toward the drive, peering over my shoulder as I screamed some more.

A loud repetitive noise from beneath me suggested Mrs. Carin had shot out a tire.

My heart raced as I wondered where the next bullet

would land, and if I was doing the wrong thing driving toward Mama's home.

The familiar *Whoop* of a cop car's siren sent a fresh flood of hope through my core, and I crammed my foot against the accelerator, jamming it to the floor.

I barreled onward like the devil was chasing me, two tires on and two tires off the smooth drive.

Mama and Eli were on the porch, eyes wide with shock and confusion as I spun out near the steps, barely missing the fountain and ATV parked nearby.

Behind me, Officer Anthony stood outside her cruiser, lights flashing, and removed the gun from Mrs. Carin's hand.

## CHAPTER TWENTY-TWO

*T*he days that followed Mrs. Carin's arrest turned Cromwell upside down. No one had thought her capable of doing any of the horrible things she'd done. I suspected she'd even surprised herself a little. The newspaper images of her in handcuffs, escorted from Officer Anthony's cruiser to the police station, started a chain of wildfire-grade gossip I was sure would burn the whole town down.

When my friend Bonnie, heard what had happened, she called to congratulate me for helping capture Flint's killer. She suggested we work together again sometime, like we had when my ex was killed several months back. And I thought I heard her boyfriend, the sheriff, growl in the background.

Thankfully, things had settled as follow-up articles were printed each day. Wilhelmina worked double-time to deliver the facts as they came available, and the town, in turn, traded morbid curiosity for heartbreak. A beloved member of our community had done the unthinkable, and she likely wouldn't be back anytime soon.

I had mixed feelings and regular nightmares about the whole thing. So I'd thrown myself into something to keep my mind off it. Something guaranteed to make me happy. And something I could control.

"Who knew a miniature donkey wedding would bring out this many people on such little notice," Mary said. "I still can't believe you managed the majority of these plans in ten days. Or that you talked me into this." She raised a finger to the wildflower crown on her sleek black hair.

I blinked, a little stunned myself. "It's been a good day."

Jack and Jill's ceremony had gone off without a hitch. Nana Hams had recommended a pet boutique in New Orleans called Furry Godmother for help with the bridal party. I purchased a dozen floral crowns for Thelma and the hens. When the owner, Lacy, heard I was on a tight budget, she talked me through the process of turning an old lace curtain into a veil for Jill. I promised to visit her shop if I was ever in New Orleans, and she vowed the same if she ever came to my part of Georgia. She sent a package the next day addressed to Jack. The box contained a top hat and tails for the groom and a whole host of gourmet spreads from a company named Grandpa Smacker. The card was signed by Lacy and her husband, apparently also named Jack.

I'd made a new friend and saved a fortune. Luckily, I'd anticipated a crowd and spent the saved cash on extra food.

Mary tugged the long pink ribbons trailing down her back from her crown.

"You look beautiful," I said, still adjusting to the sight of my grumpy friend in white cotton.

"I look beautiful every day. And I hate costumes."

"It's not a costume. It's a bridesmaid gown, and Jill picked it out, so be nice. It's not cool to disagree with the bride." I stripped off my apron and smoothed the fabric of my matching dress. "I think they're pretty."

"You would." Mary filled a tray with clean glasses and a

fresh pitcher of sweet tea, then raised it from my café's countertop and walked away.

I followed with a tray of fresh breads, rolls and Grandpa Smacker spreads.

The sun was bright and the breeze warm outside the café. I smiled at a multitude of guests and friends. It seemed the same texting app Mrs. Carin had used with nefarious intent also worked wonders to send wedding invitations.

Eli appeared as I unloaded the last of my breads and spreads onto a table with chatting guests. He'd returned the newlyweds to their pen for some alone time after all the hoopla, and his eyes locked on me as he approached.

"Thanks for doing that," I said as he arrived at my side. "I could tell they were getting antsy." It'd been a long day and a whole lot of people for a pair of donkeys who rarely visited with more than Eli, Mary and me.

"It's no problem," he said. "I set their wedding attire on your patio step in case you want to preserve any of it for posterity." He made a crazy face, and I laughed.

"Appreciated."

His grin sent a shiver of delight through me, and my smile widened in response.

"How are you holding up?" he asked.

It was a question he'd asked me every day since Mrs. Carin tried to kill me.

And my answer remained the same. "Okay."

He nodded, and I knew he'd ask again tomorrow. I also knew he'd be there to listen when I was ready to talk about it.

"Anything else I can do?" he asked.

"Not unless you know how it went at the hearing yesterday. I still have so many questions." I'd wanted to be there, but the timing was terrible. I had so much to do in preparation for the wedding. And truthfully, I hadn't been prepared to see Mrs. Carin again just yet.

Eli snorted. "You would." His eyes rose over my shoulder, tracking something in the distance. "Looks like you might get your answers."

I turned to see an unfamiliar SUV park in the field with dozens of other vehicles.

A shapely brunette climbed down from behind the wheel, long waves reaching past the shoulders of her form-fitting pink dress. She closed the door with one hip and waited while a man with sunglasses and a beard joined her at the tailgate. He pulled a big cardboard box into his arms, and she closed the hatch.

"Is that Officer Anthony?" I said, jaw sinking open. "Holy moly, she cleans up nice."

"Yeah. That's her husband, Greg," Eli said. "We met when I was stuck at the station for three days. Real nice guy. He's a third-grade teacher."

I shook my head, temporarily stunned. "There weren't any photos of him in her office."

"The photos are mostly her friends and sisters. She keeps a slide show from her wedding as her screen saver."

I turned back to face Eli, scrutinizing his casual expression. "You learned all that from three days in a jail cell?"

He shrugged.

"I knew you for a year before you did more than nod and frown at me."

"Louisa?" Officer Anthony's voice turned me on my toes. "Eli," she added. "This is my husband, Greg."

Greg nodded, but his hands were full. "Sorry we're late. My niece's birthday party was this morning. We came as soon as we could."

"And we brought a gift," Officer Anthony said. She motioned to the large, unwrapped cardboard box in Greg's hands. "It's an enrichment experience," she explained. "We stuffed it with hay, apples, pony nuts, carrots and some other treats. Our minis have a lot of fun foraging for the little prizes."

"Is there somewhere I can put this down?" Greg asked.

Eli stepped forward. "Let me."

Greg shifted the gift into Eli's arms.

"Want to check out the pen we just finished?" Eli asked.

Greg rubbed his palms together, and the men walked away.

I tried not to stare at the beautiful woman before me. "You have miniature donkeys?"

"Three." She nodded. "Greg grew up on a farm with them and several miniature ponies. If you ever have any questions, he's a wealth of knowledge, and he loves to share information. They're a hobby but also family. They bring us a lot of joy."

"I inherited Jack and Jill from neighbors who moved. I'm learning as I go."

"Well, the wedding was a nice touch. Maybe a little over the top, but certainly appreciated." She motioned to masses of Meadowbrookers and Cromwellers mixing and laughing.

"It was a success," I agreed. "I'm glad you could make it. I'm sorry I drive you bonkers sometimes."

She gave a long breathy laugh. "You keep me on my toes, that's certain. And you're doing a lot to support my favorite wine store."

I laughed.

"Have any pressing questions today?" she asked.

I raised my brows. "Really? It's not even my birthday."

"It's your donkeys' wedding day, so that's close enough," she teased.

I took her up on the offer before she could change her mind. "How did things go with Mrs. Carin in court?"

"Good for us. And as they should've for her. Mrs. Carin confessed to everything. She used Mr. Flint's phone to write the poor review of Souffle the Day because she was jealous and losing business. She was already in some financial trouble, so the loss caused by your café's opening hit her harder than she was prepared to deal with. When she learned about all the time Flint was spending here, and that he'd planned to write an article encouraging folks to check out Souffle the Day, she assumed things would only get worse for her. The scathing article didn't cause you to lick your wounds and disappear into your community as expected, and that got the snowball rolling."

"I ran into her when I was in town looking for Wilhelmina or Mr. Flint. I think she was following me then."

Officer Anthony nodded. "She was surprised to see you in town and feared what you were up to. But her plan to make sure Flint didn't write a nicer review to make up for her bad one had already been in motion. She'd dropped by the café and unlocked your back door so she could return and put the soy in the fridge. Once that was in place, she was free to invite him out here again, pretending to be you. She used the town app to bring some witnesses for good measure, all while she was at The Weathervane with plenty of witnesses to that as well."

"It's all so awful," I said. "She told me it'd taken all her time to stay ahead of things."

"Desperate people do desperate things."

"She knew about his allergy," I said, working through something else that had been bothering me. "Did she understand the severity?"

"No. She only knew that anytime he ate at The Weathervane he'd ask for clarification on whether there would be soy in anything he wasn't certain about. She assumed he'd get sick. Nauseous. A little vomiting or maybe diarrhea. And she hoped he'd blame your food."

My stomach tightened, and my heart broke for her. I liked to think Mrs. Carin wouldn't have taken the same path if she knew Mr. Flint would die.

"Once he died, and you started poking around, she lost herself. She flattened your tires. Stole Dirk Yoder's phone and orchestrated the syrup situation. She sent the binoculars and ruined your takeout order, which, by the way, I didn't realize was for me. Thank you for the thought."

I sighed and offered a sad smile. "Eli spoke with Jim the day Mrs. Carin was arrested. He admitted the package might've been mixed in with a large number of boxes from The Weathervane. Though, he still wasn't sure."

Officer Anthony nodded. "She didn't realize he saw her drop off her deliveries. And I'm guessing she had no idea he was the designated Meadowbrook deliveryman. She probably assumed all her things would pass through a half-dozen mail carriers' hands before reaching their destinations."

The low rumble of male laughter pulled my eyes to Eli and Greg on their way back to us.

I smoothed my expression, pushing myself to remember this was a party. "Can I get you something from the café?" I asked when the happy couple was back together. "If you're hungry, there's a fruit and veggie buffet, plus cakes and covered dishes inside."

Greg curved his arm around his wife. "What do you think, Katie?"

"Katie?" I repeated, testing the cute little name against the imposing officer I'd known. Then against the stylish, happy woman before me.

Her expression hardened on me. "Katie to him. Officer Anthony to you."

"Right," I said, palms popping up in a show of innocence. "Of course."

"Officer Sexy," Greg said, pressing a kiss to her cheek and pulling her into an embrace. "Let's get you something to eat, tough-guy."

She seemed to melt under his attention, then giggled as they walked away.

"Enjoy the party," I called after them.

Eli folded his arms. "They're kind of fun, huh?"

They kind of were. Who knew? "I had fun working with you on this wedding," I said. "And even though you didn't approve of my meddling, I liked getting to know you better while working on Mr. Flint's murder case."

"Oh yeah?" he asked. "Any chance we can keep hanging out? Even if someone isn't trying to kill you?"

I grinned. "Absolutely."

Though some strange part of me already missed the adrenaline highs I'd lived on while sorting clues and dodging a killer. I could see why so many people went into law enforcement. The rush was addictive.

Eli frowned, shoulders straightening. The idea he'd once been a soldier rocked back into mind.

Where had Mama gotten that information? Was it true?

"Mrs. Eggers," he said, stepping away as Mama appeared.

She wore a white linen sundress with a taupe belt and sandals. Large-framed sunglasses covered her eyes, though she was obviously staring at Eli. "Careful, Fogle, your blind spot is showing."

I scowled at her and whatever that meant.

He tensed impossibly further. "Ma'am."

"Be a dear and get me a bottled water."

His eyes flicked to mine, then he was in motion. "Yes, ma'am."

I fought the urge to stomp, complain or toss my hands up.

Instead, I went with, "Hello, Mama. You look lovely, and I'm glad you could make it. Now, what was that about?"

Her neatly manicured brows rose above the designer sunglass frames, and she clasped her hands in front of her. "What do you mean? It's hot, and I'm thirsty."

"I mean, you chased him off," I complained. "Why did you do that?"

Mama didn't answer.

We stared at one another for several long beats.

She was the first to crack. "I think he likes your attention a little too much for anyone's good."

"That is none of your business. Is that what you meant by his blind spot showing? You were talking about me?"

"I was practically on top of you before he noticed. If I was an assailant, you'd both be dead."

"Why would you be an assailant? This is a wedding reception. You're not upset that I didn't notice you."

"You weren't trained to notice."

I wrinkled my nose. "What are you talking about?"

Mama's lips parted. "Sweetheart, how much do you really know about your friends?"

"Enough," I said as confidently as possible, while my mind whipped up lists of all the things I didn't know about everyone in my community.

I looked toward the café, making sure Eli wasn't on his way back. "You offered Eli a position at Laurelwood as your head of security. Why do you need security, Mama? And why ask Eli if you don't trust him? Surely you can just put an ad in the paper."

"Why not just announce I'm low on security? Why not leave the doors open at night and hope someone comes to close them?"

My eye began to twitch, and I wished I'd opted to include wine on the reception menu.

I forced myself to focus. "You'd trust Eli to protect Laurelwood but not me. What did you mean he was trained to notice things?"

Eli reappeared outside the café, a bottle of water in each hand, smiling and chatting with a couple on his way back to our sides.

A grin broke across my face when his laughter reached my ears.

"My goodness." Mama sighed. "That is why I don't trust him with you. You've already put half your heart on a platter for the big oaf, and he doesn't have a clue."

Heat rose in my cheeks, and I snapped my attention back to her. "You want a big oaf to lead your security team?" I whisper-hissed the words, feeling my temper rise.

Her lips fell into a bland smile and her head tipped slightly over one shoulder. "Sweetie, no. I want a former Secret Serviceman."

My mouth opened.

"Two waters," Eli called, taking the final few steps to our sides. He passed one bottle to Mama and offered the other to me. "I thought you could probably use this."

"I can," I croaked. And seriously, why hadn't I ordered wine?

"Now, Eli," Mama said. "About my recent break-ins."

Eli's gaze swept to mine, but I was frozen, a half-full bottle of water in hand. My thoughts forming a hurricane inside my head.

"This time, the deviant left a note." Mama hooked her arm in Eli's and led him toward my cottage. "I was hoping you had time to talk."

I stumbled along after them, hanging on every word as adrenaline filled my veins once more.

My next case was already underway.

Thank you so much for reading my book! I'm beyond thrilled to share the Thelma & Louisa Mysteries, and the Bonnie & Clyde Mysteries with you. I hope you'll enjoy each story more than the last and that you'll keep in touch between the books!

For monthly updates on Thelma, Louisa, and my other cozy worlds, become part of my COZY CLUB NEWSLETTER!

And if you're ready to see where Thelma & Louisa got their sleuthing starts, pick up BURDEN OF POOF, book 1 in the Bonnie & Clyde adventures.

## ABOUT THE AUTHOR

Julie Anne Lindsey is an award-winning and bestselling author of mystery and romantic suspense. She's published more than forty novels since her debut in 2013 and currently writes series as herself, as well as under the pen names **Bree Baker**, **Jacqueline Frost**, and **Julie Chase**.

When Julie's not creating new worlds or fostering the epic love of fictional characters, she can be found in Kent, Ohio, enjoying her blessed Midwestern life. And probably plotting murder with her shamelessly enabling friends. Today she hopes to make someone smile. One day she plans to change the world.

# ALSO BY JULIE ANNE LINDSEY

**Thelma & Louisa Mysteries**

Out of Cluck (Book 2 of 3)

**Bonnie & Clyde Mysteries**

Burden of Poof(Book 1 of 8)

**Patience Price Mysteries**

Murder by the Seaside (Book 1 of 3)

**Seaside Cafe Mysteries**

Live & Let Chai (Book 1 of 7)

**Cider Shop Mysteries**

Apple Cider Slaying (Book 1 of 3)

**Christmas Tree Farm Mysteries**

Twelve Slays of Christmas (Book 1 of 3)

**Kitty Couture Mysteries**

Cat Got Your Diamonds (Book 1 of 4)